MY
NAME
IS
JOHN

Thomas D. Eno

Covenant Communications, Inc.

Published by Covenant Communications, Inc.
American Fork, Utah

95 96 97 98 99 00   10 9 8 7 6 5 4 3 2 1

Library of Congress Cataloging-in-Publication Data
Eno, Thomas D., 1952-
      My Name Is John / Thomas D. Eno.
            p.   cm.
      ISBN 1-55503-770-4
      1. John, the Apostle, Saint--Fiction. 2. Bible. N.T.--History of
Biblical events--Fiction. 3. Christian saints--Palestine--Fiction.
I. Title.
PS355.N65M9   1995
813' .54--dc20   94-45947
                                                       CIP

DEDICATION

To the real John. Though I have never personally met him, through writing this novel I have felt closer to him and more appreciative of his labors. His courage and dedication to serving our Lord, Jesus Christ, has increasingly inspired me.

Also to my dear wife, Laurie, whose faith in me, and in my ability to complete this story, has kept me going through all the hard times.

ACKNOWLEDGMENTS

I would like to thank the following for their help in bringing to pass this work: Gayle Leavitt Gardner, our first reader, for her encouragement and suggestions; Kurt Bendixsen, for his legal advice; and my sister, Teresa, for her computer assistance in preparing the manuscript for publication. Their assistance was invaluable.

PREFACE

At the close of Christ's mortal ministry upon the earth, John, one of the twelve apostles, made a strange request. His desire was to stay alive upon the earth until the second coming, and "bring souls unto Christ."

The modern world, and in particular the secular world, does not believe that normal aging can be suspended. Most people, if they think about it at all, believe that the actual translation in the book of John means something other than what it says.

Modern revelation (3 Ne. 28:6; D&C 7) confirms and clarifies that John was indeed blessed to remain upon the earth as a ministering servant. It is logical to assume, then, that he has been involved with the lives of people through the many years since, and that he could be among us even now.

The following fictional account does not purport to be an exact portrayal of John. The attitudes and behaviors represented are the author's personal impressions. Yet it is logical to suppose that the character of John, as represented, would be similar to Jesus Christ, who was his mentor, his leader, his friend, his Savior.

Still, who could write the life of those who knew the Savior personally? And so, with much humble prayer, seeking for the inspiration of the Spirit of God, this story was written.

Perhaps if it could have happened, it might have been like this . . .

Chapter One

The wind came up slowly. The cool autumn air began to take on a strange, silky quality that wrapped itself around you like walking through chiffon curtains. Farmers putting their fields to bed for the winter looked up and wondered at the sky. Old widows who loved the birds and spent hours watching them noticed changes in their flying friends, and worried. Young children felt the change on their bodies and in their hearts, and kept on playing.

A current of warm air came out of the south and began to push back the colder atmosphere, further and further, until finally the cold air mass fought back. At first there were only small pockets of skirmish here and there in the ocean of air, the tension building, until at last a full scale war began. Wind lashed the land with fury and the skies filled with clouds. Lightning, rare for this time of year, split the sky with flash after flash that lit up the darkening horizon as thunder filled the hills with booming echoes. Sheets of rain washed over the little community nestled in the valley below.

By now, most people had taken cover from the storm. A few curious and brave souls stood under eaves and watched the drama unfolding above. After a while, as the night came and darkness covered all, lights came on for a few hours, until all slept beneath the battle above. And the storm continued on.

Each army in the sky fought with all its might, giving no quarter.

Time stood far off and waited. The most sensitive and perceptive hearts might have felt that heaven and hell were battling over this place, over the folk that lived there. Then, as suddenly as it had begun, it was over. The cold was vanquished for a while longer by the warmth, and peace once more sat down to watch over its children.

It could have just been another late-in-the-year storm. Something to talk about for a day or two and then forget. It could have been, but it wasn't. Something was going to happen. And things would never be the same again.

* * *

The stranger picked up the broom and began sweeping the sidewalk in front of the store. There were piles of wet leaves and debris up and down the street, but no place more so than in front of Templeman's General Store.

Wedged in the space between the brick storefront and the sidewalk was what looked to be most of the leaves in town. After a while the stranger could see that this job was going to take more effort than he had thought it would as sweat began to trickle down his brow. A little music might help, he thought, as he began to whistle something that sounded like it came from another time, another place.

Seth Templeman looked out his store window to see a whirlwind of sweeping going on and wondered, "Who in the world . . . ?" Opening the store that morning, he had noticed that last night's storm had blown most of the pile of leaves that Widow Hamson had spent all day yesterday collecting down the street to his place. He had grumbled that she shouldn't have waited to bag them up; now they were all over his storefront.

But here, look at this fellow cleaning up the mess out front. Hadn't Seth always said that more people needed to take notice and help others out? Not that the town of Crystal didn't have good people in it, but most people did their own work and left others to theirs. Besides, this didn't look like anyone that Seth knew. In a place as small as Crystal, living there for fifty-two years meant you knew everyone, and the person at the end of the broom wasn't any one of them.

Part of Seth wanted to step right out and ask who the man was, while another part said to wait until the job was through, and then find out. No sense in losing out on free labor when you could get it!

Seth watched as the stranger worked steadily and noticed the man smiling as he swept. In fact, every now and then the happy sweeper would burst into song. Darnedest thing Seth had ever seen, someone who looked to be just overflowing with joy at working.

Maybe he's one of those mental patient types that drift through here every once in a while, thought Seth, glancing slightly toward the counter where he kept a loaded revolver. I better be careful. Trouble was, the stranger didn't look like he had that kind of problem. So who or what was this man, then?

The stranger was just about through with the job when Seth came out the door. Still unsure how to approach him, Seth ran his gnarled old hand through his thin, gray hair and stared. The stranger smiled over at him but didn't stop working.

When he finished up the sweeping and put the broom back up against the storefront where he had found it, the young stranger wiped his sweaty brow with the sleeve of his chambray shirt, then sat down on the curb. Seth watched him for a few minutes more, noticing the stranger seemed to be listening for something, then Seth cleared his throat loudly and ambled over.

"You having a good time?" asked Seth.

"You bet! It's been too long since I've been able to do some real work," said the man.

Seth looked up and down the street and frowned at the clutter left by the storm. "That storm left quite a mess."

The stranger smiled and turned to look up at Seth. "Sure was nice of you to leave this job for me," he said. "I needed to work the kinks out some. Besides, you probably had inventory to finish up."

Seth nodded and launched into his "I can talk to anyone about anything, because that's part of running a general store—knowing people better than they knew themselves—" routine. "Work is the best tonic for what ails most folk. In fact," he began, then suddenly remembered something. The thought changed him, and his friendly face darkened. His long, narrow nose tightened up, and his eyes closed into suspicious slits. The reason he hadn't swept the sidewalk himself this morning was because the inventory had run over last night and he wanted to finish it before the shipment from Richland came in this morning. Now, how did this fellow know about that?

Seth looked him over more closely and saw a pleasant-looking young man who looked to be about twenty, or maybe twenty-two years of age, with longish brown hair. He was dressed in jeans, denim jacket, a chambray shirt, and sandals. He wore no jewelry or watch. Nothing really all that special about him. No, wait . . . maybe it was those eyes of his. They looked like they belonged to someone far older and more experienced with life than a man this young could possibly be. No one shy of sixty could have eyes like that!

"Haven't seen you around before," probed Seth.

"Haven't been around before," said the man as he stood and offered his hand. "My name is John. I'm glad to make a new friend this morning."

Seth got flustered. He had been in the middle of some major suspicious wonderings, but rather than come across like a complete idiot he decided to drop it for now. "Where are my manners?" said Seth. "Now say there, young man, I'm glad for your help! My name is Seth Templeman. Welcome to Crystal." He took John's hand and shook it with determination.

John smiled a smile of such warmth that it startled Seth, a smile as if Seth were his best friend. "Like I said before, this is what I needed right now, so maybe I need to thank you," said John.

"Well, thanks anyway, young fellow. You saved me a lot of work. Not that I couldn't have done it myself, mind you. I may look old, but I can still work harder than most people your age."

The phone rang back inside the store, and Seth turned automatically toward the door to go in. Then he stopped as he thought of the kindness this stranger, who owed him nothing, had just done. "Wait a minute and I'll get you something to eat, if you're hungry."

"No thanks, I'm fine, Seth. But you might tell me where I could find some work. I can do just about anything."

The phone kept ringing as Seth turned back toward John and slipped back into his cautious businessman thinking. He weighed this strange fellow in his mind. "Well, you might try down at Larson's Feed and Grain. They had a hired man there for a while. I heard he made a lot of fuss in a fight at the tavern last week. Guess he didn't get enough exercise at work! Anyway, he quit yesterday, claiming the work was too much for his back—though if you ask me he's just looking for a reason to do nothing and still get paid for it. People nowadays. I don't know."

John turned to look down the street and said, "Thanks, I'll go talk to them." Turning back to Seth he said, "I wouldn't worry about getting that inventory done. I'll bet your shipment doesn't come in until late. So long." Then John turned and started off down the street toward the poorer side of town.

What shipment? thought Seth. What is he talking about?

The phone seemed to ring even louder now. "Say, don't you need some directions to the mill?" he called after John.

John stopped and turned back just long enough to holler, "No, I figure just across the railroad tracks is where it will be. Thanks anyway." Then he was off down the street, whistling a quiet, dreamy tune.

The phone kept ringing and demanding that someone answer it. Seth couldn't hold so many things in his head at once, so for the moment he put aside his questions about the odd stranger and hurried into the store. Picking up the phone and answering, "Templeman's General Store," he found out what John had been talking about.

The voice on the other end of the line was the shipping clerk at TransWay Shipping. "Whatta you mean you can't get here until late?" Seth shouted. "I got orders already set for that stuff!" There was more talking on the other end, and a deepening frown on Seth's face until he finally said, "All right, all right, I'll be waiting. But just remember, I don't make any money standing around twiddling my thumbs, you know. . . . Yeah, yeah I know. I'm sorry, too. Good-bye." He dropped the receiver down and stood at the counter for a while, glaring at a stack of macaroni bags.

"Guess maybe that guy, John, was right about things being late," he grumbled to himself.

Coming around the counter, he started to continue the inventory list when it hit him—how in the world had John known about the shipment? All his previous suspicions came flooding back and swept Seth over to the front window to see if John was anywhere in sight.

Chapter Two

By the time Seth looked out the store window, John was out of sight around the bend, almost to the tavern. The Happy Time Bar wasn't a place where you went for a happy time. In fact, you were more likely to feel worse after being there for a while. The outside of the place was painted over in layers of peeling colors that all clashed with each other. Half the windows were boarded over. The inside was gloomy and dark enough to hide all but the worn tables and chairs scattered around the place. The only real light was behind the bar, and it put a reflective glow on the bottles along the shelves there but didn't reach very far out to the tables. The stale stink of cigarettes, old beer, and a faint odor of vomit filled the place.

John would not have known all this, but Harry Morse knew it very well. Harry went there often, got drunk, and just as often got thrown out by someone he had picked a fight with. Harry was just taking another trip out the door when John came by.

Leading with his face, Harry hit the pavement with a sickening thud and skidded across the sidewalk on his shoulder, over the curb, and into the street. "That's the last time you tear up my place!" yelled the barman. "You can take your business someplace else!" Then he turned on his heel and went back inside.

John, who had stopped just short of the tavern doorway when Harry came sailing out of it, went over to pick up the injured man.

Harry had some serious bruises, and one nasty gash on his face that was bleeding heavily. "Here, let me help," said John. Harry was considerably bigger than John, so it took some maneuvering to get him up off the street. There was so much alcohol in Harry that his legs wobbled like those of a sailor on a ship in the middle of a hurricane.

"Leave the bum in the gutter where he belongs," boomed a voice from behind them. John turned, with Harry half-draped over him, and saw two angry-looking men standing there. "I said, leave him!" growled the larger of the two.

"He needs help. He's injured," said John quietly. Looking for some glimmer of compassion in their faces, he found none.

"What he needs, kid, is to get his butt kicked some more so he'll learn some manners."

The large man, whose bulky arms and shoulders strained against an old sweatshirt, smelled strongly of whiskey. He clenched his fists as he came toward John, stopping only half a step away. His face was twisted in anger, and his eyes glowed with bloodlust. It was clear that unless John put Harry down and moved on, he too would be in for trouble.

John looked into the man's sullen eyes and felt no fear. "Why don't I just apologize for whatever he did to bother you, and then teach him about manners later?"

The big man muttered something about "wise guy" and then threw a quick punch that caught John square on the jaw. John staggered back a half-step, shook his head a little, smiled ruefully, and said, "Okay, now I'm sorry for both of us!"

The smaller of the two men spoke now for the first time. " What do ya know, Jake," he laughed as he slapped the larger man on the back. "You finally found someone that can take one of your punches!" His companion turned to glare at him, intimidating him back into submission. "Shut up, Willie," he growled.

"So you think you're a tough guy, huh?" Jake asked as he turned back to John. He came forward at a rush, with every intention of ending things once and for all.

John wasn't afraid for himself as much as he was concerned about getting Harry some medical care. There just wasn't time for all this dancing around. So when Jake came close enough, John put out his hand. A bluish-white streak of light arched between them for a split second, and Jake went down like he'd been shot. He twitched, then was still. John looked at his attacker's companion, who was stunned by what had happened. When Willie met John's eyes, he stumbled back a couple of steps and fled into the bar, abandoning his unconscious companion on the ground.

John readjusted Harry, lifting Harry's arm across his shoulders and placing his other arm around the injured man's waist. As they moved away from the bar, Harry roused himself enough to stare unevenly at John and mutter, "Who 'er you?"

John smiled and replied quietly, "My name is John, Harry. I've come to take you home."

Their progress was painfully slow as they lurched along the street. Harry kept staring at John through blurry eyes, trying to figure out who was helping him. "I don't know you," he mumbled.

"Well, God knows you and He's a friend of mine. So just be a good guy and help me get you home."

By the time that John and Harry came around the corner of the block where Harry lived, his wife, Janet, was looking out her kitchen window. She was washing dishes that had been left from her small lunch, looking for things to do while she worried. Her hands were busy, but her mind kept going back to the same thing. Harry always told her not to worry about him, that he was too lucky to have anything really bad happen to him. Still, as his wife, she felt it was her place to be concerned for him. And during the last six months she had found ample reason—her husband's dwindling sales income, the growing pile of unpaid bills, and the baby that was growing within her. To make things worse, he also came home more and more often with alcohol on his breath, sometimes even sporting a black eye or a puffy lip.

Despite the deep frown on her face, Janet did not look old enough to have a sixteen-year-old son. After nineteen years of marriage, she still looked enough like her high school yearbook picture to have graduated last year. If anything, she seemed to grow more beautiful with the passage of time, despite the hard years with Harry.

"Where is he this time?" she wondered aloud as a great wave of tiredness reached up, trying to pull her down. A stray lock of her shoulder-length auburn hair came loose from where it was pulled back and hung down in front of one eye. Absently she blew it over to the side with a puff of breath.

Standing in the sunlight that came through the window, she thought back over the years with her beloved Harry and the dreams and hopes that never seemed to come true. She wondered if they would ever know peace again. He had always been so charming, so full of life, so confident, so sure that things would eventually come together. But that had been before the trouble with their son, Nathan.

She was jolted out of her thoughts when she noticed someone moving along the sidewalk half carrying, half walking with somebody. She didn't recognize the one man, but the other looked familiar. She strained to make out who it was.

"Harry!" she exclaimed as she saw his face. The dishrag had hardly hit the counter by the sink before she was out the front door of their house. By this time John and a mostly unconscious Harry were coming up the walk to the front steps.

"Harry! Oh, Harry," said Janet softly as she came to him and gently touched his bruised and bleeding face. Tears began to flow down her cheeks.

"Let's get him to bed, Janet," suggested John. Janet nodded slowly and began to lead the way into the house. Part of her wanted to just hold him and cry, but another kept her going, kept her being responsible. She hardly noticed John, who seemed very sure of what to do for Harry just now.

When Harry was upstairs in his room and laid on the bed, Janet could hold the tears back no longer. The fears and worries of the past months flowed out of her, and she sank down on the floor next to the bed holding Harry's hand, sobbing. John watched her for a moment and then left the room, returning with a washcloth, a basin of warm water, and various medical supplies he had found in the bathroom.

By the time Janet had stopped crying, John had most of the injuries on Harry's face cleaned and tended to. Then he carefully looked over the bruises on Harry's side. Harry was going to be very sore, but there would not be any permanent damage.

John came around the bed, and taking her hands, gently brought Janet to her feet. "He's going to be all right. Tomorrow he'll feel awful, but everything will heal in time." Janet looked into the eyes of John, whom she had never seen before, and found in him greater compassion than she had received from people she had known for years.

"God loves you and Harry very much," John said softly. "Do you believe that, Janet?"

She didn't know why, but Janet already instinctively trusted John, and she had always trusted God. She nodded, and then asked, "Are you a . . . friend of Harry's?"

John looked at Harry for a moment, smiled, and said, "Harry is more than a friend to me. He's more like a brother." He turned back to Janet, took her hands in his, and said quietly, "I need your faith now, Janet. Will you let me give Harry a blessing like you read in the Bible about Jesus doing?"

Janet suddenly seemed surrounded by a bubble of warmth and light that took all the uncertainty and fear from her; it didn't matter how John knew about her Bible reading. The desire in her heart for the peace of God the scriptures promised spoke for her and said, "Yes."

John turned, and stepping to the side of the bed, put his hands on Harry's brow. His words were gentle and kind, yet filled with power and assurance. Harry's body began to relax, and the last of the worry in Janet was replaced with a hope and confidence that tomorrow would somehow be all right.

* * *

Jake Skoggins woke with a start, taking a swing at nothing in particular. He sat up on the sidewalk, growled something about "jerk," then muttered a long string of obscenities. He climbed unsteadily to his feet, looking for Willie, who had long since gone inside to lose himself in a large bottle of whiskey. Jake's whole body ached. It was even worse than after the time he got drunk and tried to wrestle old man Floyd's bull.

Jake wasn't sure how he had ended up on the ground. He wondered what kind of a punch that kid had. He hadn't even seen it coming. "Probably wearing brass knuckles," he muttered.

For a moment he regretted the whole matter with Harry and the stranger. Then his pride jumped up and demanded that Jake make somebody pay for this insult to his reputation. He was, after all, the toughest guy in town. It wasn't much of a claim, but it was all he had. "That kid is gonna wish he hadn't come to Crystal," Jake swore. He turned to go back into the bar, then stopped. What if someone had seen what had happened? Jake swore again and decided to leave instead. "When I get my hands on that guy, he's going to wish he was already dead!" Walking gingerly to ease the ache in his side, he headed toward the rundown shack he lived in.

Chapter Three

A bag of wheat sailed out of the semi-trailer onto the loading dock. There was already a sizable pile there, and more kept coming. If you listened closely, you could hear a slight grunt before each one-hundred-pound bag shot out of the trailer. The man inside was perspiring heavily despite the autumn cool, determined to finish the job.

Business at Larson's Feed and Grain was steady enough to take care of the large family that owned and ran it. The Larson clan had been in and around Crystal for nearly one hundred years, though most of them seemed to move away to the big cities these days. This part of the family, led by Terrell Larson, was a close-knit group. Terrell and his wife, Shirley, had five boys and three girls, ranging from twenty-four to five years of age. Each of them in turn worked and helped out somewhere in the business operation.

Terrell reached down, hoisted up, and threw out another grain bag. He had been working on the load for about an hour, ever since the forklift broke down. His twenty-four-year-old son, Jimmy, who was his right-hand man, had gone off to locate a part for the forklift and had not yet returned. Terrell knew that Jimmy was no slacker and would get back as soon as he could. A good kid, thought Terrell.

He reached over to pick up another bag, and wrestling with it for a moment, his grip on it shifted and the bag's weight suddenly flipped to one side. Terrell felt the slightest twinge in his right lower back. He walked forward and muscled the bag out of the trailer onto the load-ing dock. Then, taking off his work gloves, he carefully felt around in the muscles of his lower right side.

Terrell was in great shape for someone fifty-one years old. Except for his wife, Shirley, who was only forty-five, he was able to work just about anybody into the ground. He had always prided himself on being able to work "harder, longer, and with less rest" than anyone in Dacome County. On the other hand, about two years ago he had been roughhousing with his sixteen-year-old son, Matt, over who was going to go through the front door first on the way to church one Sunday, and Terrell tore a muscle that seemed to take forever to heal. It still bothered him.

Terrell felt that same muscle in his side complaining now. He wanted to ignore it, as he had tried to do the first time he injured his back. At that time, Shirley, who had watched him resist getting older for twenty-five years now, told him he was being a "fat-headed fool," but Terrell had gone back to work against the doctor's orders. Next thing he knew he had found himself doubled over with pain, unable to get his breath because all the muscles in his right side had tightened down on him. It took a lot of muscle relaxant, pain killers, and bed rest before he was able to get going again.

"RATS!" said Terrell loudly, which was about as close to swearing as he ever came. He looked around at the large pile of grain bags that still lay in the trailer waiting to be hefted out onto the loading dock. Some days no matter what you plan, it all falls apart, he thought. Half-heartedly he tried to pick up another bag of wheat, but quickly gave up as the twinge in his side escalated into a severe pain that threatened even greater revenge if he didn't stop right then.

Terrell resigned himself to not finishing the load as he headed over to the office. Just then, someone behind him spoke out. The man stood just inside the end of the trailer, so there was darkness on his face when Terrell turned to look. That's strange, thought Terrell, I didn't even hear him come around.

"Guess you didn't hear me before," the stranger said. "I asked if you might have some work available."

Terrell walked over to the end of the trailer. He saw a smiling young fellow in a denim jacket and jeans. "I might have," said Terrell.

"What can you do?" While he waited for and listened to the answer, he quickly surveyed the stranger.

"Well, for one thing," replied the young man, "I can unload this trailer for you so your back can take it easy." He smiled, and Terrell smiled ruefully in return.

Although on the outside Terrell looked like a stern and distant person, on the inside he was extremely warm and friendly. Shirley always said that he had the biggest bark and the softest bite of any old dog she knew. So after a quick initial check of this stranger, he just naturally opened up.

"My name is Terrell Larson. My family and I run this crazy business." He extended his hand to the young man and was rewarded with a firmer handshake than he had felt in some time.

"My name is John. How about I get started on those bags of wheat for you?" Without waiting for an answer, John walked back into the trailer and began throwing out the bags.

Terrell watched John work for a moment, then walked off and into the office. "Got *another* new man, boss?" asked his daughter, Teresa, when he came through the office door. Teresa was more or less the office manager for the business, and though she was only twenty-three years old, she did a good job keeping her dad straight on the dollars and cents of life. She had come home from college with a degree in accounting and taken over the financial end of the business from her mother, who had done it for years. Sometimes, though, Terrell wondered just who was the boss anymore.

"Now Teresa, don't start on me about that all over again. He feels to me like a good guy." Terrell quickly turned to leave the office rather then get into a hassle with Teresa.

"Dad," her voice called from behind him, "you promised!"

Terrell stopped in his tracks, took a slow breath, and turned to face what his other kids called the "Office Monster." "I can use someone to help out since Larry got hurt and quit last week," he offered in his own defense.

Teresa got up from her desk and walked around to stand squarely in front of her dad. She was a good foot shorter than he was, but you would never have known it by the way she stared him in the eye. Looking up at him, she said insistently, "When you put me in charge of the office, you said I was to keep track of the expenses and make recommendations on how to improve the financial structure of this business. The one suggestion I made that would most change things for the better, you just keep refusing to see."

Terrell reached down and took Teresa's little hands in his big calloused ones. "Honey, I know, we've talked about this before. But he's just one guy, and he needs work. I feel that the Lord has blessed us with this place to do more than make money. Sometimes you just have to help other people out, even if it makes your own life a little harder. Don't you think that's what the Savior would do if He were here in my place?"

Teresa's jaw tightened as she wrestled with what her father said, then she turned and walked back to her desk. Picking up a pile of bills, she turned back to her father and waved them at him. "I just wish the Lord could get those farmers to pay their bills on time!"

Terrell started to reply, when he heard a voice behind him, "Where do you want those bags now?" As Terrell turned around toward the dock, John and Teresa saw each other face-to-face. Teresa saw another employee they didn't really need, and John saw someone who was frightened and overwhelmed, but refused to admit it. The scowl on her face had the beginnings of lifelong wrinkles and unfortunately cast a cloud over all the good in her.

"Just stack them neatly on the pallet, and we can use the forklift on them later," said Terrell.

"I did," said John. He smiled at Teresa with a twinkle in his eye. "And I promise I'll last longer than the others have," he added.

Teresa gave John a forced smile before turning back to her papers. Terrell peered out the doorway and saw the bags already stacked neatly on the pallet. Meanwhile, John had quietly picked up a broom and started sweeping the far dock area.

"I'll be darned," said Terrell as he walked over to the pile of grain bags. "How did he get all those stacked so fast?" He turned to look around for John, but could only hear his whistling off somewhere.

He had started to follow the whistling when another daughter, Cindy, who ran the farm supplies store part of the operation, called him over the intercom. "Dad?" came the tinny sound of her voice as it was amplified over the outdoor speaker.

"What do you need, Cindy?" hollered Terrell.

"Dad, there's a call for you. It's Mrs. Turnsen—she says she needs to talk to you right away."

Terrell mulled that over for a moment and then said, "How about you take a message, and . . . I'll get back to her as soon as I can. It's probably on that late shipment of chicken feed she's wanting to complain about." He decided to look at the first grain elevator where he thought he might fix the old ventilator that was acting up again. But before he got very far, his daughter's voice came blaring over the loading dock again.

"Dad, Mrs. Turnsen says she wants to talk to 'Bishop Larson.'"

Terrell stopped and instinctively reacted with, "Okay, I'll be right there" before it dawned on him what it meant. As the bishop of the LDS ward there in Crystal, he was used to taking calls from the members while he was at work. There always seemed to be some crisis, or maybe only a worry that someone was contemplating having a crisis over, that needed to be talked over. How often he had encouraged the ward members to trust their own ability to receive inspiration, and yet they still leaned on him. Sometimes he felt like telling them, "When I'm not around, tell yourself what you think I would say, and then do it!" Shirley, however, had told him none too gently that he probably wouldn't like what people would claim were his thoughts, and she knew that the Lord wouldn't. She also said that if he wanted to have an easier life than that of a bishop, he shouldn't have joined the Church those fifteen-odd years ago. Shirley always did have a way of getting right to the truth of things.

The funny thing about this call was that Henrietta Turnsen wasn't even a member of the Church, nor had she ever shown any interest in becoming so. In fact, when Terrell had been called as bishop three years ago, and word got around Crystal as such news always does, she was the first nonmember to talk to him about it. She had been a customer of his ever since he took over the Feed and Grain sixteen years ago; and until his calling, their relationship had always been strictly business. Then one time, as he was delivering feed for her large chicken operation, she brought up the subject.

"So you're one of 'em?"

Terrell had turned from unloading the feed bags into her barn to see her standing behind him, her hands on her hips. She was seventy-nine years old even then, but with enough energy to wear out most of the help she hired. Ornery as they came, she paid her help well, but was the terror of the valley as a boss. Most of the laborers wouldn't go anywhere near her place. She stood there in knee-length rubber boots, flannel shirt, coveralls, and a straw hat. Her face held a quizzical and amused look that might have come off one of the roosters she was always complaining about. Only five-foot-two-inches tall and weighing no more than ninety pounds, she seemed never to have figured out that she was not a large person. Everything Henrietta Turnsen did was large. Especially her fiery temper!

"One of what?" Terrell asked.

"One of those religious types!" she snorted. "I hear you're a preacher now, though why anyone with half a brain believes in all that religious hogwash I'll never know."

"I'm not exactly a preacher," Terrell had replied with a smile. "I'm just someone that enjoys going to church."

"I hear you're a Mormon. In fact, I hear they made you a bishop. So how come you're still throwing chicken feed around here for me if that's true? Guess your church don't pay very good, does it?"

Terrell had laughed, and then said, "To tell you the truth, Henrietta, the way I get paid for being a bishop has nothing to do with money." He had talked with her about the Church for the better part of an hour that day. At the end she had straightened up and declared, "Well it's no skin off my nose if you want to believe such a load of bunk, but don't try to get me to believe it. All this God stuff is nonsense. Everything I got in this life I got for myself. So you just keep being a feed and grain man for my chickens, and we'll get along fine." Then she had slapped him on the back and marched off. They had never talked about anything even remotely concerning the Church since that day.

Now, at Henrietta's persistence, Terrell put aside the old ventilator for another day and walked back into the office past Teresa, who was now buried in her paperwork. He hurried into the corner room where his desk was and tried to find the phone under the clutter that always seemed to live there no matter how he tried to keep things neat. When he found it under the pile of forms for the new fertilizer bags they were going to order, he pushed the intercom button, asked Cindy which line Mrs. Turnsen was on, then picked up the phone.

"This is Terrell Larson. Can I help you, Henrietta?" he said.

From the other end of the line came the familiar cackle, but Terrell heard a strange, subdued quality behind it. "You still a Mormon bishop?"

"I am. Do you need one?" Terrell said, trying to figure out what this was about.

"I want you to come out here," ordered Henrietta. She paused, then asked again in a quieter, more humble tone, "Would you come see me tonight, Terrell? I would very much appreciate it."

Something was very different about the tough old woman, different than he had felt before. "Sure I'll come, but why do you need a Mormon bishop?"

"Well, I've been . . . sick for a while now. And my doctor says . . . well, he says . . . Oh hell, I'll just spit it out! The old quack says I'm dying." She added more quietly, "I guess pretty soon I'll be talking with God, and you seem to know Him. So I thought . . . well, could you come over tonight?"

Chapter Four

John sat on the edge of the loading dock with his legs dangling over the side. The evening had come early, as it always does each fall. His breath became frosty clouds in the rapidly cooling air, and he buttoned up his denim jacket more securely against the cold. With a practiced eye, he searched out the constellations of stars in the skies, noticing how different they could be depending on where in the world you were looking at them from. Each place, he thought, has its own night sky view, each place has its own bit of heaven to live beneath.

His emotions and thoughts ran deep, deeper than any casual observer could possibly have realized or understood. He had traveled so many miles in his long lifetime, talked to so many people, witnessed so much unhappiness, and experienced so much struggle—enough for a myriad of lifetimes.

I didn't really know what I asked of Him, thought John. My only desire had been to serve. He sighed and felt a moment of infinite heaviness before looking up into the sky above and saying quietly out loud, "Nevertheless, not my will, but Thine be done." Then he smiled as if to say, "I'm okay now, just had a moment of wistfulness there!"

Terrell Larson came out of the office and saw John sitting alone. There was a quiet peacefulness about John that Terrell could feel and very much liked. Since being called to be a bishop, Terrell had come to realize even more that each person had their own particular presence. Some people might wear expensive clothes and possess great wealth, but still gave off a sick, unhealthy feel. Some seemed to suck at the very life force of those they met, as if a great emptiness within them sought to steal the vitality in others to hold off a growing decay and death inside themselves.

John seems so . . . so good, he thought. I wonder if he might be a member of the Church. I guess I need to find out more about him.

John turned at that moment and looked at Terrell with a knowing smile. Terrell suddenly felt very small, very young in the presence of this young stranger, who somehow was neither strange nor young. Terrell shook his head at these contradictions and ambled over to John.

Sitting down on the edge of the dock next to John, Terrell said, "You did a good job today, John. Since you're new in town and will hopefully be working for us for a while, I was wondering if you had a place to stay tonight?"

"I was just thinking on that problem when you came out. Know anybody that might have a room they could rent me for a while?" John asked.

Terrell thought over the places in town, then had an idea. "We have room at our place. That is, if you don't mind a crowd of people buzzing around. Of course it's worth the trauma because my wife, Shirley, is the best cook around."

John shook his head slowly with an impish grin. "Well, I can only accept your offer if my need to pray at every meal won't be a bother!"

It was Terrell's turn to tease. "I think we can put up with that habit. We have a little interest in praying ourselves."

He laughed and slapped John on the back in genuine friendship. Then the two men jumped off the dock and went over to Terrell's ancient pickup. It always sounded like it would fall apart at any minute, but kept fooling everyone and plugging along. Over the racket of the ancient truck, the two men shared a laughter, warmth, and just plain ease that grew with every mile they talked and traveled that night.

* * *

Shirley whistled a bit of song that she was only partially aware of. Seven o'clock was drawing near, which meant that the Larson clan would be coming together for the big meal of the day. Cooking was her favorite thing to do, even when it meant making enough for her own private army.

Terrell had built her the kitchen of her dreams, and though she never said much about it, she always glowed whenever she was in it. Out of her kitchen had come most of the prize-winning jams, jellies, preserves, cakes, pies, you name it, at the Dacome County Fair each year. Now as she made the final meal preparations, little Amber, the youngest of the Larson family, climbed up on the step stool to get the plates from the cupboard to set on the huge oak table that dominated the dining room.

Shirley had heard from Cindy that Terrell had hired another man, and that even though Teresa was mad about it, he seemed to be nice enough. Shirley's intuition had also told her this meant someone would be coming for dinner. She would get after her husband for not calling ahead, he would apologize and promise to call from now on, and then the time would come that he would show up unannounced with yet another soul to be fed. It was a well-acted-out performance that the whole family understood and accepted. After these many years, Shirley still adored her husband, so whatever gruff scolding she might give him never amounted to much.

The signature whines and rattles of Terrell's truck coming down the lane reached Shirley's ears about the same time that her two sons—twelve-year-old Randy and nine-year-old Boyd—came crashing down the stairs past the kitchen and out the back door yelling, "Dad's home!" She smiled and thanked God in her heart for the love her children had for their father, and he for them.

Shirley strained to see out the kitchen window, while at the same time continuing to peel carrots for the salad. The mercury vapor light that lit up the driveway out by the barn showed her husband getting out of the truck and with him, another man. The stranger paused next to Terrell, who waved his arm around and pointed out back behind the barn as the boys ran around the truck and back toward the house. Probably giving the ninety-eight-cent tour, thought Shirley.

Boyd and Randy came stampeding back into the house and began to wrestle next to the dinner table until they upended one of the chairs. "All right, that's enough, you two. You go get washed up, pronto!" ordered Shirley. Both boys stiffened up into mock soldiers and saluted her until she came out of the kitchen and grabbing them, began some serious tickling. Then they ran off at high speed, giggling nonstop, toward the downstairs bathroom at about the same time that Shirley met Terrell and John coming through the back door.

"Mrs. Larson," boomed Terrell as he came in, "this is John." John came through the door next, nodded his head to Shirley and said, "It's nice to meet you." Terrell leaned over and gave his wife a kiss. "I brought him home for dinner," he mumbled, then quickly went down the hall to the bathroom. Shirley smiled at John and said, "Please make yourself comfortable, we'll be having dinner in a few minutes." She shot a sharp look at her beloved husband's retreating back and then followed him down the hall out of sight. John heard something about, ". . . still not giving me any notice, are you?" some silence and then laughter. John could tell that he might not have been fully expected, but that he was welcome anyway.

* * *

After dinner, Terrell and John took the old pickup truck out to Henrietta Turnsen's chicken farm. As the truck bumped along Hartley Road, John felt just a little uncomfortable, what with all the food he had packed away at dinner that night. It had been a long time since he had enjoyed eating, and those he ate with, so much. Good food and good conversation, topped off by good company—the best of times!

John's thoughts went back to the many nights like this one, when the twelve of them had followed Him. How many times He had taught them, joked with them, cared for them late into the night. We never knew how short and how precious those times were, thought John. We were blessed beyond measure and never really knew it until He was gone.

Wham! The truck hit a huge pothole, jerking John roughly back to the present. The ancient engine moaned in complaint at the abuse and doggedly kept on going. "Sure appreciate your coming along," hollered Terrell over the noise. "These feedbags we're taking out aren't all that heavy, but with that storm coming in as fast as it is, I'd just as soon get home early before it hits. That forklift breaking down put us behind schedule." Wham! The truck hit another huge hole. "Besides, I might need you to get out and push!"

John knew that if anybody got out and pushed, it would be Terrell who would insist on doing it, but he played along. "I could do that, all right, but I think I'd rather pray for your truck instead."

"That reminds me," said Terrell, "I was meaning to ask you about that praying you do. Do you have a particular church or something that you attend? It's just that most people these days don't seem to have much use for prayer the way they used to."

John smiled in the dark of the truck cab. He had been waiting for this conversation, and now he needed to be careful how to answer the question or things would go too fast. "I believe in the teachings of Jesus Christ, as He taught them in their purity before they were changed to make them more convenient. You and your family are members of The Church of Jesus Christ of Latter-day Saints. I am also a member of Christ's church."

"So are you a Mormon?" asked Terrell.

"You won't find my name on the records of your church, but I am very much one of Christ's disciples."

They rode in silence for a bit, as Terrell pondered that statement. John went on, "I have been baptized and confirmed. I know the holy priesthood as God's power on earth. It's not something I do on Sunday. It's my whole life."

Terrell chewed on that for a while in his mind before he heard a soft voice inside of him say, "All that John has told you is true." A knowledge greater than his own personal life experiences and understandings touched him, and gently swept aside any doubt within his mind. Terrell didn't know how John could be all he said he was and not have his name on church records, but somehow he knew John spoke the truth.

Sighing deeply, Terrell said to John, "Well, I figure myself for a pretty good judge of character. Some of the people who call themselves Mormons are sure not Latter-day Saints, the way I see it. Their hearts aren't in it; they hold back just that little bit of themselves from the Lord, thinking that without it they will lose themselves, or lose out on life, or something like that. So maybe someone like you is more a member of the Church than they really are. I don't know."

John understood how much trust Terrell must have already felt for him to be able to speak so directly from the heart. Reaching over to

Terrell, he gently patted him on the shoulder and said, "You're a good man, Bishop. I'm sure the Lord is pleased with your caring so much about your flock."

"I try," said Terrell. "Sometimes I get tired of all there is to it, but generally I feel good about my calling."

"Big job. Guess that's why you get the big bucks," kidded John.

"Yeah, right."

Wham! The truck fell into another hole in the road and almost died. "You can start praying any time now!" yelled Terrell over the coughing engine.

Chapter Five

Henrietta Turnsen and Terrell talked in the kitchen until late into the night, and John fell asleep on the couch in her front room while he was waiting. By the time Terrell and John were headed home, the storm was in full swing. It was a good thing there were two of them, one to drive and wrestle the old truck against the raging wind, and the other to act as lookout and peer through the rainswept windshield for any debris and downed tree branches on the rough road.

John spent that night and a few weeks more with the Larsons, and the bonds between them grew deeper and deeper. He felt like a member of the family, almost as if they had known each other intimately long ago, and had only forgotten it.

John grew to appreciate each of them, and to know their strengths and weaknesses, as they shared their lives with him.

The oldest, Jimmy, and his wife, Marriane, didn't live in the Larson home, but had a small apartment of their own in town. Nevertheless, they spent many evenings back at the family place. Marriane was another daughter and sister to the Larsons.

Jimmy was a returned missionary. Quiet and serious, he showed great respect and kindness to others. That was what had attracted the vivacious, outgoing Marriane to him in the first place. Underneath Jimmy's quiet surface was a quick wit and lighthearted sense of humor that often eased tensions about him. He had wisely chosen a wife who appreciated and complemented his qualities.

A gracious and talented young woman, Marriane had a sweet and generous nature, and always looked for the best in others. She had been blessed with a beautiful singing voice, and often sang at church functions. Friends and family naturally thought of her for weddings and funerals in the community. She had met Jimmy while in college, and had moved far away from her own family home to marry him. To make up for the loss, she had fully embraced the Larson family. They couldn't remember anymore what is was like before she came.

Teresa, the eldest daughter, had won a full scholarship to BYU, the result of her almost perfect academic record. She liked everything neat and orderly, both in her relationships and surroundings. One day Shirley had confided to John that Teresa had not been a very happy child. She had always wanted to be the one who decided what would be played and how the games would go. It was not a trait that endeared her to friends. On the other hand, she had been an excellent student. Memorizing things and finding how to organize vast quantities of information appealed greatly to her.

Only grudgingly did she accept John's presence. She wasn't sure why she was uncomfortable around him, except that he didn't fit into any of her preconceived notions of how he should be. Knowing this, John strived to ease the tensions between them, but wisely understood that the best thing he could do was give Teresa some space. So while he never tried to avoid her, he was careful not to come too close, either. She was the only one of the Larson family who was not immediately drawn to him.

Lighthearted Cindy, at nineteen, was on top of the world. Having just graduated from high school the previous June, she was getting things together for college. Although she had been a good student, she had never let that get in the way of what she saw as the "more important" things in life—friends, family, and finding something to laugh over each day.

At eighteen, Matt was the outdoorsman of the family. Hunting and fishing were his passions; school was not. A "C" in a class was good enough for him, except in auto mechanics and PE, where he excelled. Matt was happiest when he was left alone to work, and he loved to hear the purr of an engine that had started out as a mess.

Though only average in height, he had inherited his father's broad shoulders and strong arms, which had been improved upon with years of weightlifting. He had been the pride of the Valley Football Conference, sacking the opposing quarterbacks an average of four times per game. He had retired as only the second person to be state heavyweight wrestling champ for three years straight.

Then there was Lee, actually Leland. Named after his mother's favorite brother, Lee was tall, six feet four, slender and slow moving. Blessed—or cursed, depending on who was looking at it—with unruly strawberry blonde hair, Lee usually covered it with a green ball cap. While a bright kid, Lee was content to stay in the background at school. Unlike Matt, Lee was definitely not athletic. He was extremely shy and found it almost painful to say much to anyone; Shirley was about the only one who could coax things out of him. Lee was also discovering girls. Not those things called sisters, but real honest-to-goodness GIRLS! Nevertheless, he was too shy to do much about it except be miserable. His mother had some concerns about him in that area, but his father had told her not to worry. After all, look how he, Terrell, had turned out. Shirley had grinned, "That's what worries me!"

Randy at twelve and Boyd at nine were hard to talk about separately, since they were like two peas in a pod. If ever there were kindred spirits, they were. Both were computer game fanatics as well as baseball addicts who knew the batting averages of every active player in the major leagues. Shirley liked to joke that although she was the one who had gone through all those months of pregnancy, somehow the two boys were both the spitting image of their father.

And finally, Amber. The surprise child, the bonus gift from God, as her parents called her. Bright-eyed, Amber missed nothing. At the same time she was hesitant to speak to strangers, and chewed on her braids when she was nervous. Shy and sensitive, Amber would cry silent tears when she was sad, her face turning crimson with sorrow and pain. And yet she was the queen at giving hugs to members of the family who were struggling with something unknown to anyone else.

John came to know them all, and to love them. He had come from a large family himself. Being with the Larsons, well, it made life a little bit easier.

* * *

John and Terrell were working on the still complaining fork-lift.

"Terrell," said John, "would it be all right if I took an early lunch? I noticed a room for rent nearby that I want to take a look at."

Terrell stopped working on the forklift to look over at John. In the past few weeks he had grown to love this young man like his own son, or maybe like a brother. He always felt better around him, and he felt that the spirit of God was with him. So he wasn't really in a hurry to see him live someplace else.

"You getting tired of Shirley's cooking?" asked Terrell. "She'll be heartbroken when I tell her!"

"Actually, it's your snoring at night that's the problem," John teased back. "You rock the whole house!" They both laughed, then John said, "No, it's just like I said before, there are some things I need to do in my life that are easier when I live alone."

"Yeah, I understand . . .," said Terrell. He put his head back inside the forklift, started banging on something, then paused before saying, "The truth is, John—you're a snob!"

John heard some soft chuckling from within the forklift and leaned down, putting his hand on Terrell's back. "Of course," John mused aloud, "if I could figure a way to stuff some socks in your mouth at night, I might be able to stay at your place!"

Thirty minutes later, John had rented a room with a shared bath at a clean but run-down house on the south end of town. It hadn't been easy. The owner, Homer Ballshide, was a wizened old retired bachelor who had lived in the large Victorian style house all of his life, having been born in the master bedroom when it had been a private residence.

He treated his house as if it were a person and didn't let just any-one off the street rent a room in it. He wanted only those who would treat his house with loving kindness and respect, as he did. His house, and the people he rented to, replaced the wife and family he never had.

Homer talked with John for a while, and when he found out that John had been living with the Larsons for the past couple of weeks, loosened up his reservations considerably. He had heard about the "new man" at the Larson Feed and Grain, all favorable. Homer had known and liked Terrell Larson from when Terrell was just a little shaver. If Terrell liked and trusted this young man enough to take him into his home, then by golly, so would Homer.

He gave John the only room he had available, the smallest in the place. The one way up on the third floor, around back. Homer didn't usually rent that one out. It was cold in the winter and hot in the summer. He told John that, but the young fellow said it didn't matter. So, okay. After they had talked a little while, just to be sociable, John excused himself and went on his way.

Walking back to work, he went past Seth Templeman's General Store. On impulse, he decided to stop in and say hello. He had run a few errands over to Seth's store from time to time for Terrell, and had come to know Seth a little better, as well.

Seth was tall and lanky, with a silver head of hair and a small bald spot on the top (which he was quite sensitive about). He had told John how he and his wife had planned to sell the store when he reached sixty-five, buy a motor home, and take off for parts unknown exploring the country. Then two years ago, just before Seth's sixty-fourth birthday, his wife had been cleaning off the top shelves in the back of the store when she had suddenly slipped and fallen off the step stool. It hadn't been much of a fall, but when Seth reached her, she was unconscious. Rushed to the hospital, she had died without regaining consciousness, and the doctors had told Seth that she had suffered a severe stroke. It had probably been the stroke that caused the fall, and in the fall, she had struck her temporal lobe and her brain had hemorrhaged, causing her death before anything could be done to save her life. It had devastated Seth. He had lost the person who had been the center of his life and heart for thirty-four years.

And so, he had explained to John, that was the reason why an "old codger" like him was still running a store. What else did he have anymore?

As John opened the old-fashioned heavy wood frame front door, running his hands gently over the fancy carved contours, he noticed how unusual it was these days to see such effort put into carpentry, and wondered who had taken the time. He was going to ask Seth about it, but noticed Seth arguing with someone at the counter. Not wanting to intrude, John wandered down one of the aisles, half listening and half browsing among the wide variety of things stacked, piled, and clumped together all over the place.

"I don't care," exclaimed Seth. There was some low grumbling from whoever it was at the counter with him, then Seth said again even louder this time, "I don't care! You may have bought it here, but you abused it and now you want me to pay for your stupidity. Get out, and take your worthless gun with you!"

There was a bang and then a huge crash. John walked around a stack of rubber boots near the store counter to find Seth Templeman being held up in the air by his shirt collar, his feet dangling inches above the floor. Struggling and turning redder by the moment, he was no match for the large man who held him captive.

"Please set him down," said John with a quiet firmness.

The angry man lowered Seth until his feet were back on the floor, but he did not loosen his grip. Then he slowly turned to look at John. It didn't seem possible that Jake Skoggins could become more angry, but when he saw John his eyes widened, and his anger from the fight he had lost added fuel to his current rage.

"Hello, Jake. Are you having a problem with my friend Seth here?" asked John with a smile as warm as Jake was cold.

"Stay out of this," snarled Jake. "First I take care of this cheatin' old man. Then I take care of you!"

John calmly walked over to where Seth was gasping for breath and began gently but firmly removing Jake's fingers from Seth's shirt. "Jake, it just seems like you and I keep having these meetings. Maybe God's trying to tell us something. Why don't we sit down and figure out what it is?"

Jake tried to resist, but the power of John's efforts to release Seth were just too much. Almost like he was in a trance, Jake watched his fingers being pried off of Seth, who quickly retreated behind the counter, gagging and shaking.

Jake didn't like being treated like that. Up until a couple of weeks ago, he had pretty much been top of the heap as far as he was concerned. He had always taken pride in his superior size and strength, and if people feared rather than respected him, well, that was just fine. He thought it made him important that others got out of his way, and he became frustrated and angry when someone did not. Particularly since nearly everyone always had, always did.

Then this "weird" drifter had shown up. Now Jake was being laughed at behind his back all over town. Like all bullies, Jake had instinctively known immediately when he was losing control of his world.

The hesitation in Jake lasted for only a few seconds before he came to himself, and bellowing like a bull, charged at John. Jake never saw John quickly step to the side before the stack of canned peas was in his face. Cans exploded in every direction as Jake crashed through the stack and went down. He rolled over onto his hands and knees and slammed away whatever got near him.

Seth had finally overcome the choking from Jake's attack on him. He yelled, "You get out of here before I call the sheriff!"

Jake ignored Seth and whirled around to face John. This time there would be no hurried rush, no blind attack. Jake was a bully, but he had the instinctive reactions and understanding of a street fighter. He now realized that this stranger would take more effort to beat than others he had easily overpowered.

Seth picked up the phone to call the sheriff. Jake reached over and grabbed the receiver out of his hand, tearing the cord out of the wall and tossing it away. Then he backhanded Seth to the floor before turning to face John again.

John stood in front of the cellar stairs, quiet and calm. "None of this is worth your anger, Jake. It's time for you to quit living with your fists. Why don't we find another way to work things out instead of doing it the same old way?"

Jake curled his lip and swore under his breath. Then everything seemed to happen at once. Seth came up from behind the counter with a loaded pistol, pointed it at Jake, cocked it and started to pull the trigger. John leaped to stop him, crying, "No, Seth!" At the same moment, Jake leaped for John, who just a moment before had been at the top of the cellar stairs, and with John no longer there to block him, kept going right on down the stairs.

There was a loud thump, then another, and then Jake lay at the bottom. John quickly ran down the stairs to kneel beside him. "Just lie quietly," he said. From the top of the stairs, Seth muttered, "Good! Let the skunk lay there until the sheriff gets here." Then he left for the gas station across the road to use their phone.

Jake came around some and tried to move. A wave of pain and surprise came over his face. "I can't move my legs," he gasped.

"Your back is broken, Jake, but I can help you if you let me." John tenderly brushed the hair away from Jake's eyes and waited for a response.

Jake had fought all his life against what he saw as a world that didn't care if he lived or died. His motto had been "Do it to them, before they do it to you." Twice he had tried to destroy this man who now offered to help him. He still would not have let his walls down had it not been for the awful pain in his back. Just the tiniest part of his heart opened up and said "Yes," and that was all John needed.

John put one hand under Jake and the other one on Jake's forehead, then he closed his eyes. Jake heard a few whispered words, something about "Heavenly Father . . . healing . . . atone . . . Jesus Christ." As John opened his eyes, there was a different feeling in that dusty cellar room. A spirit of peace and love had replaced the anger that Jake had invited. Jake had not been able to understand most of what John had said, but he began to feel a burning sensation in his back. "What did you do to me?" he cried.

John reached over and, taking hold of Jake, began to rise up with the 240-pound man, holding him like he was a little child. Carrying him over his shoulder, John carefully took Jake up the stairs and deposited him against the counter just a moment before Seth and the sheriff came in the door of the store with a deputy close behind.

"Okay, Jake," said the sheriff tiredly, "let's go for another ride down to my office. Looks like you're going to spend some more time down at the jail." Smiling encouragingly, John reached out and took Jake's hand to pull him to his feet. Jake stood up unsteadily, swaying slightly as the deputy placed handcuffs on him and escorted an unusually quiet Jake into the back seat of his car.

Seth was talking to the sheriff while John quietly left the store. He locked eyes with Jake through the car window for a moment before Jake looked away. When Jake looked again, John was gone.

Chapter Six

Three days after the incident with Jake Skoggins at Seth Templeman's store, John was working late. He had volunteered to finish up an order that was to go out early the next morning. "Bishop" Larson had hurried off to a church meeting, and everyone else except Teresa was gone for the day.

John stacked the last feed bag into the truck and sat for a moment to rest on the stack. A bit of light from the mercury vapor lamp over the dock area made its way into the back of the truck, but other than that it was dark and quiet in the early winter evening.

Another light from the office just barely came through the layers of smudge that had built up on the window. John knew that Teresa was holed up with her ledgers and numbers and probably would stay that way until late into the night. She seemed to take a particular pleasure in grinding out more and more numbers. John thought that it was small solace for the pain and loneliness he knew was in her heart.

He knelt down there in the dark of the truck for a few moments of prayer, then got up and began walking slowly toward the office. His face showed that he was thinking intently, until it all came together in his mind. Then he smiled easily, picked up his walking pace, and began to whistle a tune that seemed to be a cross between "Swannee River" and "I Am a Child of God."

Teresa was muttering to herself about a column of numbers that wouldn't add up right when the door of the office opened and John came through. She looked up, and recognizing that it was him said, "Sorry, just me here!" before returning to her figuring. She hoped he would take the hint and go away, but he didn't, so she focused even more intently on her work and prepared to wait him out. For the past two weeks he had been trying to make conversation with her, and she had just as definitely been giving him the brush-off. John nonchalantly went over to the invoices for tomorrow's deliveries and thumbed through them for a few minutes, then walked to the chair by the wood stove and sat down.

Teresa carefully stole a glance at John. She didn't want him to know that she even cared if he was there, but his eyes met hers as he sat across the room smiling at her. Teresa shook her head and quickly looked back at her figures. She was irritated that John was still there, and even more irritated that he might see that he affected her enough that she was irritated about his presence. She was confused by John. She couldn't figure him out, so his presence affected her in strange ways— ways she didn't understand and couldn't control very well. And what Teresa couldn't control or understand, she didn't like. Why didn't he just leave her alone?

"Cold out there," said John. "I sure am glad to get near this stove!"

Teresa mumbled, "I suppose so," without looking up from her work. For a few moments she forgot he was there as she finally found the numbers she was looking for. Numbers were so comforting, so dependable.

"I hear your father's birthday is next week," came his voice from by the stove.

"What? . . . oh, yes it is."

"How old is he going to be?"

"Huh . . . what? . . . oh, he's uh . . . going to be fifty-two."

It was silent for a moment, and then John's voice again interrupted Teresa's figuring. "So which day is it on, exactly?"

Teresa stopped what she was doing, set her pencil down hard on the desk, sat up ramrod straight in the chair, and with a loud squeak of protest from the old wooden chair she was sitting on, swiveled to face John. Her face was set hard, her eyes cold, and she was determined that this was absolutely the last exchange she was going to allow this night. "My father's birthday happens to fall on Thanksgiving this year. Thanksgiving is always, by tradition, the fourth Thursday of November, so it follows that his birthday will be next Thursday." She paused for a moment and then continued. "I have been informed that there will be a special dinner celebration in his honor. Since you are apparently well liked by my family, I suspect you will be invited to attend and will know exactly what time all this will occur as well as I will."

While Teresa was talking, John's grin had grown even wider, and his eyes twinkled. He was obviously enjoying the conversation, which Teresa had not failed to notice.

"Now, is there anything else that you just can't go on living without knowing?" Teresa asked curtly.

"I'm afraid there is, Teresa," John said with mock solemnity. "Why do you try so hard to act tough and hard?"

"What?" gasped Teresa. "What are you talking about?"

"You!" said John.

"Look, I have work to do and I don't have time to play mind games with an itinerant drifter who likes to imagine that he's a psychiatrist, or whatever. So if you'll just be off on your business, and let me do mine, I'd appreciate it."

John stopped smiling. Looking deeply into her eyes, he searched and felt for the right words to get past her walls. "Look, how about a cup of herbal tea? I'll make it for you myself. I hear it does wonders for the tired soul," he suggested gently.

Teresa turned back to her desk and gripped the edge of it, her hands white with tension. "Who do you think you are? You show up here out of nowhere and worm your way into everybody's life. And everyone is just supposed to open up their hearts and tell you all their troubles. . . . Well, not me! I got along just fine in my life long before you ever came along, and I don't need your help!"

Teresa was shocked to find she was shaking. What was it about this stranger that made her lose control?

John sat quietly for a moment, then got up and walked over to the kettle on the office hot plate. He poured some water into Teresa's cup, put a bag of her favorite herbal tea into it, and gently set it on the desk next to her.

Teresa had felt like exploding when she got to the end of her out-burst at John. She waited for him to come back at her, and when she realized that he wasn't going to, she began to soften some—but only a little. He seemed to see so easily inside of her, to know her better than she knew herself. He saw things in her she tried to hide even from her-self. It frightened her, and she attacked him out of fear.

When he brought the tea over, her heart wanted to say some-thing, wanted to reach out a little, to say he had indeed said some-thing of the truth about her. That she did act tough, to keep away the emptiness inside.

"I meant no offense, Teresa," said John quietly as he stood by the desk. "I only saw your heart struggling. The Spirit told me you're unhappy with your life but afraid to let anyone know, or help. I thought you could use a friend."

"Why can't you just leave me alone?" asked Teresa. Her face was full of pain, the result of years spent avoiding the truth.

"I'm not the enemy you make me out to be," he said, pulling up a chair beside her desk. John inhaled deeply, looking through the wall behind her toward distant mountain peaks he could see only in his heart. Wish though he would, trying to reach someone's heart, espe-cially when it was so encrusted with self-righteous pride, never got any easier.

Refocusing on her, he said, "I know that you aren't the tough, uncaring person everyone thinks you are. Under that drill sergeant exterior is a fragile, tender heart. I see you feeding the stray kitten that hangs around here. You make sure it gets something to eat every day. I hear you talking to it, I feel the love you give it."

"You don't really know anything about me," she protested, but her voice was softer, quieter than before. Her whole soul ached and twisted.

"No one is without failures and imperfections, no one is without some success in being alive," he continued. "Being alive on this earth means making mistakes and being imperfect."

"Oh, I make lots of mistakes," she admitted, anguished tears caus-ing the words to catch in her throat. She sniffled and dug into her pocket for a Kleenex to wipe self-consciously at her nose. "I work so hard to stop making them. I keep thinking, if I could stop making them, maybe people would . . ."

"Would what? Would love you, because you'd be perfect, you'd finally deserve love?" John asked.

"No, that's not what I meant." Startled and confused at being suddenly so exposed, she turned her head quickly away from him, ashamed of herself. It was exactly what she had thought; she just hadn't intended to say it out loud.

"Teresa?" John reached over and took her chin in his hand, gently but insistently turning her back toward him to look into her eyes.

"No, no," she protested, reaching to touch his hand, but not pushing it off. As her eyes met his, the look in his eyes was calming, healing.

"Teresa," he said, "It's all right. You're all right just as you are. This is the way we grow. You're all right with me, and more importantly, you're all right with God. He loves you as you are. You can't earn that, nor can you make it go away."

She slowly lowered her eyes, overcome with what he was telling her, hot tears washing her face, her heart on fire. Her spirit ached for release from the prison she had built for herself. Could it be true?

"You've locked yourself in a terrible place," John continued. "It's cold and dark and frightening. You have nightmares there, so you throw stones at the monsters you see around you. But can't you see," he said earnestly, taking her face in both hands, the gentle warmth and strength of his fingers reaching out to her, "the stones you throw are hurting only the other poor mortals around you. And every stone you throw becomes another stone in your own prison wall, making it ever more terrifying and difficult for you to get out."

"I don't understand." Her voice was soft, pleading, almost child-like now, afraid to believe that the door to her dungeon cell might be opening up a crack.

"No one can live up to the impossible standards you set for them. And neither can you. It's very simple. You can't get smart enough, tough enough, or quick enough not to get hurt by life. No matter how hard you try. The circumstances that are a part of life will always win. Unless . . ."

"Unless what?" Teresa sniffled.

"Unless you let God in. I mean really in. You do it the way Jesus taught, even if it doesn't seem safe or make any sense to you. And then when you get smacked in the face, because you will, you turn to God and let Him heal you. And," he added, "no tough guy attitudes, no pretending it doesn't hurt."

"I know that!" she wailed in frustration.

John continued with patient perseverance, ignoring her interruption, "When people disappoint you, you forgive them for being like you are—human. And among those you will have to forgive, remember to forgive yourself as well—for not being perfect."

John rocked back in his chair. "Why not let us love you? Open up, let us care. Life is so much better that way."

He stood easily, pushing back his chair. "I have to get going." He smiled down at her, compassion in his warm eyes. "There's more I'd like to share with you, when you want me to." At the door, he paused and said before he left, "You might try talking to Heavenly Father. I'm sure it's been a long time since the two of you had a really good chat." Then he was gone out into the night, leaving Teresa alone with her thoughts.

She stared for a long time at the closed door. Thoughts and feelings swirled around inside of her, looking for rest, and found none.

Now that John had left, Teresa realized in horror how much she opened up to him. The mask of competence and self-assuredness she had worn around him was no longer possible. With only a look, a single word from him, her fragile pretending would be shattered and lying in shreds about her feet. How could she ever face him again? How would she be able to maintain any sense of dignity around him, with what he now knew about her?

Turning back to her desk, Teresa slowly closed the ledger book. She had never really had a close friend, and it had been lonely in high school for her. She wasn't popular, no matter how many clubs or committees she might lead. Nor was she pretty like so many of the other girls she had secretly admired and wished to be like. But it was her tense and tight heart that had been the biggest obstacle to her wishes for friends. Sadly, she never saw that simple truth.

College should have been better, but it wasn't. She watched the other girls and their dates, saw them get engaged and married. No one had ever tried hard enough to get to know her. But then, she couldn't be expected to throw herself at just any man, could she? And so she had returned home and devoted herself to her work and family.

As long as I can remember, she thought, I've tried to make our family better. I'm the oldest daughter, someone that has to set a good example for the younger ones to follow. Mother's all right, but Dad needs a lot of work. He doesn't seem to see that being realistic about life is important. He always gives me that "meek and humble" routine. Well, not for me. I tried it, and all I got was hurt.

Remembering John's tender warmth for her this night painfully brought things back to the present. It was no use. His words echoed again and again in her heart. It was true, she was alone in a prison of her own making, terrified of the darkness around her. She buried her face in her hands. Tears squeezed through her eyelids as she reluctantly began to weep.

* * *

John trudged along in the cold night air, looking up at the stars and smiling. "Well, I guess that opened some things up. The Lord said it would. He really knows His business!" John picked up a rock and threw it down the road, listening to it skip and bang into other stones along the way. A dog barked and came running along to walk with John for a while and get his head scratched before heading off somewhere else. Life is good, he thought, even if you live almost 2,000 years. Of course, it's hard to keep yourself in shoes when you live that long!

John was laughing at his own joke when he suddenly felt a quiet, yet powerful impression in his heart. It was the smooth, illuminating feeling that is impossible to describe in words, but which anyone who has experienced it understands. He stopped walking and said quietly, "Yes Lord, I'll go right away." And that was that. There were no great lights, no heavenly choirs, just a gentle awareness that God was talking to him. Then, as he accepted the impression and was obedient to the call, his awareness of what to do and how to carry it out became ever clearer. He had made a habit of responding to the spiritual promptings through these many years, and his spiritual communications had become very precise.

John turned himself around from the direction he had been going and headed for Janet and Harry Morse's home. He didn't know exactly why he was going there but he knew what he was going to give them when he arrived.

Walking along the street until he came to the railroad tracks, he hopped up on the railway and followed it along for a while, listening to the crunch of the cinders beneath his shoes. In this part of town, the tracks almost seemed to shy around things, being hid behind old warehouses and dilapidated cattle holding pens from when the town was a busier place. Walking along on the dark tracks, away from anyone else and some distance from the residential part of town, John could think deeply.

Things are going the way they need to, he thought. The Morse family will be turning around soon, Seth Templeman will be rethinking some things, and Jake Skoggins at least has a chance now. Pretty full day, John old boy!

When he came around a bend in the tracks and into the light of the mercury vapor light behind the National Guard Armory, he had a sense of something up ahead; someone or something was badly hurt. As he finetuned his spiritual awareness, he was interrupted by the sound of a train whistle. He jerked his head up and saw that coming toward him was a quickly approaching freight train.

John began to run now, without any clear understanding of why. His logical mind was wondering and still gathering information before deciding on a course of action, but his heart already knew what needed to be done.

As he ran faster toward the approaching train, he saw in his mind's eye a small brown heap draped across the railroad tracks. Then the vision became more distinct, and John could see that it was what was left of a kitten that had been badly mauled.

It was going to be a race now between John and the train to where the kitten lay. The engineer blew his whistle longer and harder as he saw someone in the bright light crazily running along the tracks toward his train. John was breathing harder and harder as he ran with all his might. His body reached its limit, but still John pushed it for greater speed as his heart drove him onward to stop a needless death.

With no time left, he ran the last step and leaped for the kitten. He snatched it with one hand, pulling it off the track, and rolled away from the train. He lay silently on the rocks as the cars hissed down the tracks. The noise was deafening and the vibrations terrifying, but the kitten never moved. There was nothing to do but wait. Wait until it was over.

More than a minute after the train had finally passed, John began to stir. He rolled over on his back, blinked, and shook dirt out of his eyes as he spit cinders from his mouth. Then he stiffly got up and went over to sit down in the half moonlight on an old oil drum that lay rusting on its side in the weeds by the tracks.

John didn't expect to find much life in the little bundle of fur, and he was surprised to be greeted with a very faint but unmistakable "mew." One yellow eye opened part way to look at him and then slowly closed again. The little body was torn and broken in more ways than could be described. What life there was within was quickly fading away.

John held the dirty, blood-stained bit of yellow and white fur gently to his chest. He closed his eyes in prayer, and for a moment seemed to give off a faint glow. Then, looking down at the kitten, he began walking down the tracks again.

* * *

The little Morse home looked quiet and snug, with smoke coming from the chimney and a warm glow in the windows. He hadn't been around since last Friday when he had checked on Harry and eaten dinner with his new friends.

Someone had been cleaning out some weeds from around the sidewalk and along the white picket fence and had left them lying around on the ground and sidewalk up to the house. It'll just take a few minutes to finish off the job, John thought to himself, and taking his jacket off, he made a soft bed out of it for the now sleeping kitten. When he finished sweeping and went to put the broom back by the door on the porch, he turned to find Janet standing there without a coat on, watching him.

"Caught me in the act, did you?" John laughed. "Well, it's not what it seems. I was really trying to put the weeds back on your walk and all over the place, but I kept getting confused. Guess I'm not much good at practical jokes!" He came up the steps, set the broom down on the porch by the door, and kissed Janet on the cheek.

"You're a terrible liar, John. Don't ever get a job selling used cars." Then she put her arms around him and hugged him, saying, "I was just praying that you would come back around. We've missed you."

She looked over, and then stooped down—as well as she could with her pregnant belly—to look at the kitten. "So who's your friend?"

John reached down and picked up the now purring ball of fur. "This is an early Christmas gift for someone special."

"It's darling! I wish I had a kitten like this." Janet gently took the kitten and held it to her cheek. "Harry keeps saying that someday he will get me one. I get so lonely here sometimes."

As he picked up his coat, John smiled. "I told you it was for someone special. Merry Christmas, Janet." Taking her arm, John began to head inside. "Is that roast beef I smell cooking?" he hinted broadly as arm in arm they left the cold starry night and went into the house.

Chapter Seven

The home of Janet and Harry Morse was small, yet comfortable. The furnishings spoke of the great love there between the two of them, with something of each of them mixed together throughout the house. The furniture was old, yet well taken care of. The ancient wood stove put out a warmth that wrapped around John like a comfortable blanket. Traces of scents from rolls, roast beef, and mashed potatoes eaten at dinner earlier that night lingered in the air, adding to the feeling of comfort and home.

John finished off the leftovers from dinner that Janet had set before him and patted his belly. "That was some great meal." He put his hands on the edge of the table, pushed himself and his chair back, and leaning backward a bit, stretched. "I'll say it again, Janet, that was some fine meal." He looked over at Harry, who sat across from him at the kitchen table. "No wonder Harry looks rounder than the last time I saw him."

"Now wait a minute," protested Harry, pretending to be hurt. "Just because it's true is no reason to say it outright. Besides," he said, smiling mischievously, "Janet would feel downright unhappy if I didn't appreciate her cooking the way I do. You wouldn't want me to hurt her feelings, would you?" He reached around the kitchen table and hugged her.

Janet, who was getting quite round herself carrying their unborn child, put on a look of mock hurt and surprise. "I don't know, Harry. You told me yesterday that you were hungry enough to eat the stove if it had catsup on it. Maybe someone like that has no need for fine cooking."

John was leaning forward now with his head in his hands and his elbows on the table, enjoying the lighthearted banter of his two friends. In the course of his visits with them, he had come to understand them better than they knew, and he could see that underneath their happiness was a good deal of unresolved sorrow and fear.

As John watched Janet get up from the table and take his dirty dishes to the sink, the thought crossed his mind about how much he had wished over the many, many years, that he could have someone like her to share his life with. "Oh well, someday, when my mission is completed," he consoled himself, and set aside his own concerns in order to help his friends.

Harry suggested that they go into the living room, where they could be more comfortable. It was a treat to have John visit, and they wanted to savor it.

"So, have you heard from your son, Nathan, lately?" asked John purposefully.

A cloud of unhappiness came over Harry's face and, scowling, he squirmed uneasily in his easy chair. Out of the corner of his eye, John saw Janet duck her head and look out the frosted window next to her. With his simple question, the veneer of happiness had been scraped clean off of their tortured hearts.

"We don't know where he is. The last word we had was that he was picked up three weeks ago by the police over in Clayton City and taken to a juvenile home. But he ran away from there before they even had time to call and let us know." Saying this, Harry looked at John with such pain that he seemed close to breaking.

"I . . . there was a call from someone," Janet said hesitantly as she began to pet the orange and white kitten in her lap. It licked its paws, and began cleaning milk off its face from the best meal it had ever tasted. "Yesterday someone called and just listened on the phone for a moment before hanging up. I thought maybe it was . . ." After saying this much, Janet looked back down at the kitten on her lap.

"Why didn't you tell me?" Harry asked irritably, although he was uncomfortable letting John see the tension between Janet and him. Still, he felt justified.

Her answer came softly but clearly, "Because my heart said to wait. You always get your hopes up, and then nothing comes of it. Then you're mad. I don't want to see you hurt anymore."

Harry turned and self-consciously smiled at John. "I guess maybe I do worry too much. After all, there really isn't anything we can do about it."

"I know you're worried about your son. Most parents would be," said John. "But I promise you God knows where he is and what he is doing. Nathan is being guided as much as he will allow it, and I feel you will see him again, sooner than you think."

Janet raised her head to look at John as he was speaking and said, "I believe you, John. Sometimes when I'm praying, I feel the same thing. It's like God is telling me to be at peace and trust Him, that He knows what is coming and will take care of things, so I can leave it to Him."

Harry drummed tensely on the arm of his easy chair, looking back and forth between John and Janet. He shook his head slowly from side to side and said, "I don't know. I wish I felt as good about all this trouble with the boy as the two of you do. All I get is a gut ache worrying about him and wondering if we'll ever see him alive again." His face clouded up again. "Crazy kid. What does he think he's doing out there?"

John sat quietly for a few moments while the ticking of the clock on the wall nearby seemed to get louder and louder as the silence among the three grew deeper. "I'd like to tell you a story," he said, "about a man and his garden." Janet and Harry both looked up at John curiously. "It seems that a certain man had determined to plant a garden. It was going to be the best garden ever. He dug up the ground, got rid of most of the stones and rocks, and prepared the soil with manure. Then he planted his seeds, taking great care to put them in the ground according to the instructions. Some seeds were to be planted deep, and some needed more shallow furrows. Some were planted all by themselves, and some were bunched together with others. When he was through planting, he stood back and admired his work.

"Well, time went by and though the man watched the garden very carefully, the days seemed to drag by before anything began to come up. Finally some small, fragile plants began to emerge. The man was so happy that he danced around and hugged and kissed his wife.

"There were also other kinds of growth. Things that the man had not planted began to grow and threatened to take over the garden. So he weeded and weeded, barely able to stay ahead of the unwanted plants. He also fought bugs of all kinds that ate the young green plants and threatened to destroy them. He sprayed and kept watch over his little growing plants, determined to give them the best of care. It was a lot of work, but it seemed worthwhile to the man, because he had a clear vision of what he thought the end result would be.

"The weeks went by and the garden grew. Some of the plants that the man had planted did very well, some did so-so, and some just never got going. It was hard for him to figure out, since he cared for all the plants so much, working to keep them all healthy and strong.

"The man's wife said to him, 'Are you sure that they all need the same amount of water? Is there someone you could ask who has more experience with gardening?'

"'Watering is watering! What's the difference?' insisted the man.

"Harvest time came, and the garden was not the success the man had expected it to be. When his wife asked him about it, he said with a shrug, 'Maybe I could have done some things different, though I don't know what. I gave my heart and soul to that garden! I guess I'm just not a gardener. It seems like too much work to have to worry about.' So he gave up the garden forever, and let it become a patch of weeds."

John finished his story. For a few moments the only sound in the room was the ticking of the wall clock, and the purring of the kitten in Janet's lap.

"I don't get it," said Harry.

"It's about us, sort of, and Nathan, isn't it?" Janet ventured. "It's about looking inside yourself and seeing honestly who you are, where your weaknesses lie and when you need to ask for help. And about accepting that living things, people especially, have freedom to choose how they will grow and what they will be. That is a truth that we can either work with, or fight against and be frustrated."

"Well, the guy in the story really worked to do his best, and he didn't seem to get much good out of it," shot back Harry.

"Like Janet said, everyone must choose for themselves," said John. "What they will become, where they will go, what they will believe in. Just knowing the truth about who and what you are is not enough. Your son, Nathan, is young in years, but he knows enough to recognize right from wrong. No matter how much we may love and nurture him, no matter how well you have taught him, he must still find his own way to the right path, the one that leads to real happiness."

Janet had been sitting with her eyes half closed in a reflective mood and listening intently. Now she spoke up. "So, what you're saying is that everyone has to find the truth inside themselves and then choose to do something with that truth, hopefully to do something worthwhile and good with that truth."

"That's exactly right." John smiled tenderly at both of them for a moment and then continued. "Find the truth, trust in the truth, live the truth, and be blessed by the truth. Light, truth, love, and God. For all practical purposes, they're all the same."

Harry sighed heavily and said slowly, "That's pretty heavy stuff." He drummed his fingers on the chair arm. "But maybe you're right. Maybe even Nathan has to find the truth himself. I just wish I could have another chance with him."

No one seemed to have much more to say after that, so John said, "Why don't we have a prayer together?" Harry didn't pray much, figuring that Janet did it for the both of them. And though he felt self-conscious, he knelt silently beside the others.

"Father in Heaven," John began, "we thank Thee for the gift of truth and understanding Thou hast given us this night. Our hearts have been touched and our spirits renewed by Thy presence. Please watch over Nathan. Help him to remember the love his parents have for him. Please bless Harry and Janet to be at peace in Thee. Now, may we gain strength to live more fully Thy ways. May we trust in Thy guidance, may we put our cares in Thy hands this night and always, is our humble prayer, in the name of Jesus Christ our Savior. Amen."

* * *

Later, after John had said his goodbyes, Janet and Harry stood arm in arm in the doorway of their home and watched him disappear into the night shadows. Then they quietly turned and closed the door. Their hearts had been touched this night. And the feeling in their home was more hopeful, more positive and at peace than ever before.

Harry caught Janet on her way out to the kitchen to clean up before retiring for the night and swept her up in a hug that was more like the Harry of long ago. "How about we just go snuggle for a while?" he whispered in her ear.

Janet pulled back enough to look into her husband's eyes. "Sure you want to get close to all of me?" she asked smiling as she patted her ample pregnant body.

"Sure, best kind," he said with a wink. "On cold winter nights like this, pregnant women are better than a hot water bottle."

"Oh, you!" she protested, but there was love in her eyes as they turned and went to bed. Whatever the troubles of the world, or their own that night, they left them in the hands of God. Who, as John sometimes said, was going to be up all night anyway, so why not let Him take care of things while we get some sleep?

Chapter Eight

Thanksgiving Day finally arrived, and Terrell Larson's fifty-second birthday came right along with it. The Larson home was awash with activity. Randy and Boyd had continuously played one good-natured trick after another on John, but had never quite been able to get the best of him; he almost seemed to know their thoughts. Cindy was busy packing and enjoying the last bit of time with her family before she took off for school. Teresa was her usual self, full of ideas on how things should go and hardly able to keep from taking over in the kitchen. Shirley was entirely capable of cooking the turkey, but Teresa had a continuous flow of suggestions as to how it could be done better. It was fortunate for Teresa, and the spirit of the day, that her mother was so tolerant.

John's presence at the Larson Thanksgiving celebration put a major damper on Teresa's enjoyment of it. Ever since their talk at the office that night, she had done her best to avoid being alone with him, or even giving him an opening to say more than a sentence in her direction. The crowd at the house was a welcome way to put some distance between them. She had thought about his words, and try as she might she couldn't find a way to gracefully get by what he had said. Finally, she had decided uncomfortably that whatever he wanted to be, she was going to make sure that from here on out she would be too busy for any more talks with him.

John had tried to help out in the kitchen but had been shooed away by the women, so while they prepared the dinner, the men of the family settled down in the living room, to watch a football game on television.

Little Amanda, whose sixth birthday would be in two weeks, had a quiet face but eyes that sparkled with excitement. She alternated between going into the kitchen to look at the turkey through the oven door glass and sitting in John's lap, where she finally fell asleep despite the murmur of occasional conversation between Terrell and John as they watched the game.

Terrell gazed at Amanda fondly, and then his thoughts turned to Jimmy, who was enthusiastically involved in the game, and his wife Marriane. They were expecting their first child soon after Christmas. This would be the first grandchild for Terrell and Shirley, and Terrell was more excited than anyone. He reflected happily that Marriane, with her sparkling eyes and sweet, cheerful nature, was more like a daughter to them than a daughter-in-law. Jimmy had followed in his parents' footsteps in finding someone who was a good match for him. Whenever they were together, the young couple gave off a comfortable glow from the love between them.

Turning toward John, Terrell inquired, "So tell me about your family. Do they live anywhere around here?"

"No, they're far away," answered John. "I haven't seen them for a long time. But in some ways we are still very close."

"I know what you mean. I've got a brother who lives all the way across the country. Neither of us are big on letters or phone calls, and we don't travel around that much either. But I understand how you can still be close. When I get together with my brother, we just take up where we left off."

Terrell twisted up his face as he wrestled with a thought, then sighed deeply. "What did you tell me your last name was? I remember it was something unusual. Zeb . . . Zabus . . . "

The room erupted into spontaneous cheers as a touchdown was scored. John's focus shifted to the game for a few minutes. When the action replay had been shown several times from different angles, and the game became more routine, Terrell launched back into his questioning.

"Let's see, I was asking . . . "

"Zebedee."

"What?" asked Terrell.

"My last name is Zebedee."

"I've never heard that name before, at least not as a last name. Where does it come from?"

John smiled mischievously. "My father."

Terrell smiled patiently. "Yeah, yeah, I get it. The joke's on me! Of course, your last name comes from your father. I didn't think that you got it out of a fortune cookie. What I meant was, what nationality is it, what kind of people does it come from?"

John leaned across the couch, and putting his arm around Terrell's neck, pulled him close in a conspiratorial huddle. In a secretive tone, John whispered, "The name comes from very nice people."

Terrell just stared at John for a moment, then pulled away and sat up. "Fine! You don't want to tell me, don't tell me! I don't need to know this big mystery. That's all right!" He then set his mouth in a straight line and looked only at the football game on TV, even though he hadn't been paying attention and didn't know what was going on.

"Terrell," pled John, smiling, "it's no mystery. Every child in my family has the last name of Zebedee. It's a very old name. And as far as being unusual, well, it's not if you're Jewish."

Terrell turned quickly back to John now. "I didn't know you were Jewish. Do you . . . uh, attend synagogue? Isn't that what they call it?"

"No, I don't go to synagogue very often these days. I still find value in much of the ritual, but I've found even more good in the teachings of my Savior, Jesus Christ."

Terrell chewed on that for a second and then said, "Don't you think it's about time you came to church with us? You've been here for weeks now, and I'm running out of patience in being polite and not bothering you about it." Terrell smiled a huge smile and reached over on the couch to grab John's shoulder in a vise grip.

"But I have been going to church, Bishop," replied John, "just not the one you go to."

"You mean the ward over in Clayton City? How did you get over there?" asked Terrell.

"Actually, I've been to the Baptist and Catholic churches a few times, and once I went to the Jehovah Witness meeting." John had cocked his head to one side, a half smile on his face.

Terrell looked surprised. He took his hand from John's shoulder and said, "Okay, you're a very accepting and open-minded guy, but don't you think you should be worshiping God in the most . . ." Terrell struggled to say what he believed, and at the same time be tactful. "That is, there are some ways of worship that are more whole, more complete than others."

John was considering his answer when the call came from the kitchen to come and eat. He reached over, gently punched Terrell's arm, and said simply, "I'd like to go to church with you and your family this Sunday. It should be very interesting."

Everyone came together around the large oak table in the dining room. They all knelt together and Terrell, at the head of the table, gave the prayer. "Father, we thank Thee for all the many blessings which Thou hast given us this past year. We are able to be together, we are healthy and happy. Our finances are a bit better than last year, and we hope that Thou has more in store for us that way. We thank Thee for our membership in Thy church and the advantages that knowing the truth gives to us in this world. We thank Thee that our friend John can be with us and share in our blessings. Most of all, Father, we thank Thee for our Savior, Jesus Christ, without whom we would be lost. Please bless this food and the hands that have prepared it for us. These things we pray in the name of Jesus Christ, our Lord. Amen."

Everyone rose from the floor and sat down at the table. Teresa looked at John strangely until he smiled warmly at her, then she looked away. After their last talk, she had avoided him even more studiously than before, and he hadn't tried to follow up their conversation with another. But maybe now it was time to try again. He made a mental note to himself to make the attempt before the end of the evening.

The food, the talk, the love that was there filled their hearts and the room. Even with all the kidding, teasing, and bantering that went on, it was obvious that these people deeply loved and cared about each other. In this world of so many cold hearts, it was a joy to John to be able to share this time with them.

After dinner, it was the holiday tradition in the Larson home for the men to do the clean up while the women relaxed and talked. John volunteered to wash and soon made short work of the huge mass of dirty dishes. "Where did you learn to wash like that?" asked Matt. "I hate 'em so much it takes me forever!"

"I learned a long time ago, my young friend, that when you find a way to like what you are doing, the doing gets easier." Then he winked at Matt who wore a look of "Yeah, yeah, I've heard this before. 'It's all in the attitude!'" Despite his look, John continued, "Besides, what I do, I do for the Lord. I love Him, and I know that He loves me. Whatever I do with the desire to serve Him lets me be in His presence while I am doing it. I figure any opportunity to feel close to Him is a treat."

He paused for a moment as if remembering other pleasant times, then said, "Know this, Matt, our mortal life is but a moment, and our eternal life with God so very close. Oh, if only you could see how thin is the difference between this life and eternity! If you could, none of the troubles of this life would impress you very much."

"Yeah," replied Matt, more seriously now, "that's what Dad always says, too. But I have a hard time seeing it yet. Guess I'll just accept it on faith, for now."

John set down the plate he was washing and turned to face Matt. "You do that, my friend, and your faith will be rewarded one hundredfold. Of such faith are the prophets made."

Matt flushed with self-conscious pleasure, and renewed his efforts at the dishes.

Even though everyone kept working while John was talking, the feeling of the moment had changed. Everyone had been listening very intently, and it occurred to Terrell that it must have been like this among the disciples of Jesus. They must have hung on his words like this, spiritually aware that they were being taught eternal truth. The apostles must have . . . the apostles! Terrell stopped and turned from drying a dish to look at John more closely. Could it be? Something said it was. There were four, the three Nephites and . . . John, who were allowed to stay on the earth until. . . . No, it couldn't be. Terrell shook his head in wonder. Could it?

"Well, that's the end of those dishes," said John. "Now, let's celebrate your father's birthday." He grabbed Terrell by the arm and led him into the living room. Terrell tried to look John in the eyes, but John managed to avoid it.

"About time you slowpokes got finished," said Shirley as they came into the living room. "If you bunch had to make a living from washing dishes, you sure wouldn't get rich. It's a good thing we don't have to wait like this except on special occasions!"

Terrell was escorted to the seat of honor in the middle of the couch, with everyone forming a semi-circle around him on the other seats and on the floor. The customary birthday song was sung, almost on key, and the candles were blown out on the cake that was brought in from the kitchen, with a lot of effort on Terrell's part. In the opening of a multitude of presents, Terrell forgot about his thoughts of John. When at last all the presents had been opened and suitably admired, he stopped and said, "Thank you all. My heart is so full. I have been so blessed by the Lord. No man is any richer than I am. Thank you."

Later that evening after cake, ice cream, and some games, Terrell stood on the big front porch talking to John while Jimmy went to warm up the VW for the ride back to town. The clouds of frosty vapor from their breath floated around them. "I'll be looking more closely at that book you gave me, John. It seemed pretty interesting."

"It was just something that I have had for a long time, and has given me a lot of pleasure. It felt right to pass it on to you."

Terrell's thoughts about apostles, and John, now came back. But just as he started to ask about it, John spoke up first. "Do you want me to take that load of feed out to Mrs. Turnsen tomorrow? If I remember right, she always likes to have her orders for the next month a bit earlier than most people."

Jimmy started honking the horn on his VW bug for John to hurry if he wanted a ride back to town, and Shirley called for Terrell to come inside and help with something or other. "Sure, as soon as you come in tomorrow you can take Henrietta's stuff out to her," said Terrell a little reluctantly. He really wanted to talk to John, but he was obviously not going to get the chance right then. *I'm not going to forget this, and at some point I'll find out more,* he thought.

"See you tomorrow," John called as he jumped down the porch steps and got into the bug. Terrell watched them drive off and noticed that John was grinning. He knows, thought Terrell. He knows what I'm wondering, which says something right there! Another call came from the house and a cold wind came up. Terrell shivered, and turned to go back inside. "Getting old," he muttered.

Chapter Nine

The next morning John got to work early, loaded the feed, and was off to Henrietta Turnsen's before anyone saw him. John had plans that day for the "Old Atheist," as she had called herself. Plans that required him to be at her place before she had a chance to start her regular daily routine.

When John drove into the chicken farm about 5:30 A.M., he saw a light on in the kitchen of the house. "She should be coming out any minute now," he thought to himself. He parked the truck around back of the main shed and began unloading the feed bags onto the loading dock, listening for her footsteps.

"You expecting me to pay more because you came a little earlier than usual?" asked Henrietta.

John stopped and turned to face her. "Nope, just thought you might like it if you didn't have to stop your feeding schedule to take a delivery."

Henrietta eased just a little before catching herself. "I remember you. You're the new man that soft-hearted Larson hired, aren't you? You seem to have taken charge of things pretty quick. He doesn't usually let someone come out here on their own for quite a while."

John smiled and turned back to bringing in the feed bags. "Guess maybe he knows how much I like you," John said lightly.

"Humph!" snorted Henrietta as she looked at her watch to note it

was 6:04 A.M. "You probably just figure you can take your time coming out here, and get out of more work back in town."

John brought back in the last bag and tossed it onto the pile. He
turned slowly to look at this old woman who made such a point of
keeping people at arm's length. He knew she was actually very lonely,
but afraid to admit it for fear of letting anyone get close and hurt her.
"You know, Henrietta," he said, "just because you've been hurt so bad
by people in the past is no reason to expect everyone to be that way."

Henrietta watched John carefully now, unsure of what kind of person he was. She started to protest that he was "talking out of the top
of his hat" when he reached over and took her hand. There was a slight
prickly feeling and then everything in front of her faded into darkness.
She started to cry out in fear, but heard John say, "It's all right,
Henrietta," and a feeling of peace came over her.

After what seemed like a long time, she could make out a bright
light in front of her. Then she saw a little girl playing with an old-fashioned doll with a porcelain head and painted face. The girl was hum-
ming a song that Henrietta could not make out.

Behind the small girl stood an old gray house with a windmill by
the barn, and a great oak tree with branches that covered the whole
front yard. Somehow it all seemed familiar. Of course, it was
Henrietta's home when she was just a child!

Henrietta forgot that only moments before she had been standing
in a chicken shed with one of Larson's men. She was remembering—
or was she actually visiting?—someplace she had long forgotten. Part
of her was glad to see the old place again, and yet part of her also felt
a mixture of fear and sadness.

Her father suddenly appeared in the door and walked across the
lawn to where little Henrietta sat under the tree. He was a stern looking man with a white beard and tight face. "Come with me,
Henrietta," he said.

She pretended not to hear and kept playing with her doll. "It's
time to play our game," said the man. "The one we play when your
mother goes to town." Tears began to fall from the girl's eyes. She left
her doll by the tree and walked sadly and slowly into the house with
her father.

Beholding this scene from her past, Henrietta felt all over again the ache of the child. She knew that the "game" meant he would touch the little girl in ways that she didn't like, in ways that were wrong. Make her do things that . . . "Oh, no" sobbed Henrietta. "How could he do that to me? I loved him and he hurt me, over and over again! He was my father!" Then she began to cry uncontrollably with great waves of pain and sorrow.

"You never told anyone," said John, who was standing next to her now. "You thought no one would believe you, that they would blame you. For years you have carried shame and needless guilt. All that pain and fear. All alone, all this time. So it was easier all these years to become hard and throw up a wall up between you and others, and between you and God."

"Where was God when I was being hurt like that?" snapped out Henrietta furiously, once again covering her pain with anger.

Quietly John responded, "He was there by your side and weeping. He found no good in what happened to you."

"Then why didn't He stop it if He loves me so much?" she shot back.

John stepped in front of her and took both her hands in his. "Henrietta, you've always said that people need to learn the hard lessons of life or they never amount to anything. You have said that, haven't you?" She nodded reluctantly, recognizing that they were indeed the exact words that she had said so often. "Well, God feels the same way you do."

Great silent tears began again to flow down her face and she asked quietly now, "What lesson was in that hurt for me? I have hurt for over seventy years. Do I have to hurt like this forever?"

"Even after the hurt was done to you," John said softly, "you continued to hurt yourself many times over."

Henrietta looked at her life and saw the many times she herself was unkind to others. As she heard her thoughts and felt the pain inside herself that she carried, she understood how she took her mind off her own discomfort by focusing on the faults of others. She realized that each time she was hurtful to others, a voice, or presence, had been nearby urging her to accept help, but she had turned away.

"I became what he was, didn't I?" she murmured. "When he hurt, he took away my peace, and when I hurt, I took away someone else's peace! In my own way, I became just like him." In horror she turned away and buried her face in her hands.

John motioned for her to look upwards. "Look, my sister. Behold the love of God." She looked up, and it was as if she saw a series of pictures of Jesus—in prayer, in pain. She felt him hurt for her and knew that he had taken not only the pain of her abuse, but also the pain that she had inflicted on others all these years.

"Why?" she cried out. "Why should He do that? I haven't believed in Him."

"Because He believes in you, Henrietta," said John. "But unless you now make a choice to let go of past hurts, to give up your negative ways, and to seek to give love to others and trust in Him, the atonement He made for you will not do you any good."

Her tears poured in a torrent down her cheeks, but unmindful of them, she looked more intently upon the scene of the Savior. As she watched, the Lord faded from her view and a bright light began to surround John and Henrietta. "This is the Spirit of the Lord, Henrietta. It has come to you that your heart might heal," said John. "You must forgive the hurts done to you. Give them up to God to replace with His good. You must also accept your own wrong actions, feel them, and then release them to Him. The word 'repentance' means to fix what you can and then leave the rest to Him. But you have to ask for His help—both to heal the hurt done to you as well as the hurt you have done to others. He won't force it upon you."

Slowly, she whispered, "Help me, God! I know I've done a lot of wrong things. In my own ways, I hurt a lot of people. Please help me fix things. Please take away my pain." As she did, the light around her changed into a more golden hue, with sparkles of brilliance interspersed throughout. She let go of John's hands and clutched at her stomach, rocking slightly back and forth on her heels. After a few moments a quiet, serene peace came over her. Closing her eyes, she felt a welcome relief from the aches she had held onto for so long.

When she finally opened her eyes, she saw herself standing in the chicken shed again. The man from the feed place was stacking bags along the far wall. Her eyes crossed her watch and she saw with some confusion that it said only 6:05 A.M. "What the . . . ?" she began out loud.

John stopped his stacking and turned toward her. "Did you say something, Mrs. Turnsen?"

Henrietta was completely confused now. She didn't know what to make of what she had just experienced, and didn't feel comfortable asking this near stranger about it. *Better let it go for now until I can figure it out,* she thought.

"Er . . . you about done there?" she demanded.

"You bet," said John. "I'll be leaving now. Any message for 'Bishop' Larson?"

Before she was aware of what she was saying, she blurted, "Please tell him to call me. I want to talk some more with him." She turned and quickly walked away, but John heard her final words—"about God."

"I would be delighted to," said John, and he was out the door of the shed and gone.

Chapter Ten

A cold wind whipped around the outside of the three-story house where John rented his furnished room. It was still dark on this Saturday morning. He owned no alarm clock, but he knew that it was almost 6:00 A.M. Years of living by the seasons had attuned his own inner clock to an accuracy far beyond that of most people.

Lying with his arms folded up behind his head resting in his hands, his thoughts drifted far and wide. Tomorrow he would be going to the LDS ward where his friend, Terrell Larson, was bishop. He was looking forward to attending. Hope it goes better than the last time. he thought.

He had gone to worship previously with members of the Lord's church in these latter days and often found them less than interested in being "Saints." They just don't seem to understand that there is a difference, a big one, between being a "Mormon" and a "Latter-day Saint," he thought. It was a lot like the difference between being religious and being spiritual; the first is an outer thing and the second is inner. Spirituality is a core, a feeling, a whole way of being that directs the outer part of a person to do good things for the right reasons. Too often, people want to know what they should do rather than what they need to be. Being requires the heart, while doing can be done without giving yourself up to Him.

Last time you talked like this, he said to himself as he rose from bed and began to get dressed, the temperature got a lot cooler all around you! When he was completely dressed he knelt beside his bed and began to pray.

"Father in Heaven, I thank Thee for watching over me in my sleep. Thou hast blessed me greatly." Some time later, John arose from his prayer and considered what to do with his day. He had not been given any assignments for the day and had nothing that was left over from the week. He had been fasting since the Thursday evening celebration at the Larsons. It was very important for him to be in tune with the Spirit of the Lord when he met the congregation of Saints this Sunday. Subduing his body while feeding his spirit was a discipline that he had accepted and practiced for ages. It was easy for him to do now, and he almost never experienced any physical discomforts.

"Urrghup!" his stomached growled. "Shhh!" he whispered back to it. "Not until tomorrow."

He stood by the window for a while, looking out at the cold winter landscape. It was trying to snow, but the flakes never quite made it to the ground. No one was in sight, and the whole town seemed to be huddled at home close to many separate fires. "Nothing like a good wood fire to warm your bones on a cold day. Wish I had one here. Homer wasn't kidding when he said this room gets cold," he shivered.

Turning back to the bed, he took a copy of the King James Bible from the bedside table that a previous tenant had left. Sitting down on the edge of the bed, he thumbed through it until he came to the book of John. He read, "In the beginning was the Word, and the Word was with God, and the Word was God." He shook his head and thought to himself, Sure glad Joseph got that corrected. It was supposed to read, "In the beginning was the gospel preached through the Son. And the gospel was the word, and the word was with the Son, and the Son was with God, and the Son was of God." A lot of what I was trying to convey got twisted and turned around over the years, John shook his head.

He had taught so many of the Father's children over the years, and so few of them had understood. At times they came to "believe," but they did not "trust." They weren't willing to put their lives in His hands. They still played the worthless game that said, "I can do it by myself."

John sat meditating for a while before deciding to go for a walk. Bundling up warmly, he wrapped himself in the scarf Janet Morse had made for him. Smiling at the bright blue and gold design, he thought how much someone from Brigham Young University would approve of his scarf.

Stepping out the side door of the house, he was immediately hit with a blast of cold Arctic air that blew down from Canada. The worn leather coat of Terrell's that Shirley Larson had given him blocked most of the cold wind but he shivered anyway.

His cheeks were soon a ruddy red color as he trudged out of town past the elementary school, now quiet with no one to play on its swings and slide. He walked past the old movie house with its boarded up door and windows, only the ghosts of past memories to fill its dusty seats. Through the cold streets he trudged onward over the bridge that covered a frozen highway of water. The quiet serenity of the setting allowed him to ponder deeply on the eternal truths he had learned.

John loved people; he also loved to be peaceful and quiet. Often the two did not go together well. His life as a disciple of Christ required enough time alone to develop and maintain a close relationship with God. However, he also had to have close relations with other people. There really wasn't a great distinction between the two, he had found. Loving God was loving others, and it was also loving yourself.

He saw some tracks that looked as if a fox had crossed through the dirt along the road, and he hoped that it had found enough to eat. Funny, he thought, no one would think to ask if this fox is a "good" fox, or skillful at what he does. They would just see him as what he is, no more, no less. Yet people looked at other people and judged them according to some measure that said, "You're not measuring up, so shape up or ship out." How can there be any real comparing or measuring among incomplete, imperfect mortals when we are all so different, so unique? he pondered. All these years I have yet to meet one person who was really so much like anyone else. On the surface they might seem the same, but scratch deeper and the difference was obvious.

One of the benefits of living on the earth so long, John knew, was seeing the truth so frequently. Everyone has to learn for themselves what is real, what holds up when times get tough. He laughed out loud to himself. I love what Brigham said, "If you love the truth, you can remember it." Thing is, most people love lies or half truths a whole lot more, and they can remember them pretty darn good! Trying to get them to replace their convenient, comfortable illusions with inconvenient, uncomfortable, challenging truths was one tough sell job.

A semi-truck went by, stirring up a mini-storm of dust. John waved at the driver who didn't seem to notice. A raven flew past him and turned up a small pathway between the trees. It felt right, so John followed, soon leaving the road behind him. Here the wind was blocked and the temperature quite a bit warmer. The trees were bare of leaves, but there were many thick bushes and a few evergreens that reached over his head in height.

John liked the quiet. Sometimes all the time he spent with other people drained him, and he needed to get away by himself. A wave of tiredness came over him, and he sat down on a log to rest. Closing his eyes, he soaked in the peacefulness of the place and the moment.

His mind wandered freely as bits and pieces of his life floated before him. Some were pleasant, and some not so.

The memory of a clearing in the woods, not unlike the one that he was now in, though in a much warmer climate, came to him. It was about thirty years after Jesus had ascended into heaven, and John had been teaching a group of followers. There were a great many people, old, young, women, men, and many children. John couldn't quite remember just where or when it had been, but it didn't really matter that much. He had such experiences many times, and many places. This memory was just one of many that haunted him.

"What are you saying?" asked a large man with a full dark beard. His face was flushed and he was obviously upset at something John had said. "We are the children of God, He expects us to be busy with His work. The kingdom of Heaven cannot be built if we do not do it!"

John stepped down from behind the rough hewn pulpit and walked toward the man. Putting his hand on the man's shoulder, he spoke to him gently, "My brother, God is pleased with the good work you do. But he is also pleased with those who enjoy the beauties which he has put all about us. God is a joyful God, not a God of sour, heavy laboring. It is no sin to work hard, and to be happy and enjoy life."

The man pulled himself away from John. He was silent, but he had not changed his mind at all. John had started to speak again when a woman stood up.

"You speak to us as if we know not the truth. We are not as the Jews who rejected the truth Jesus offered them. You ask us to accept those who play and waste the time they could be working, those who do not take seriously the importance of this mortal life. The prophet Joshua said to 'choose whom you will serve.' We have chosen to serve God, and the labor of our hands shows that."

John had paused to listen for a moment to the sweet sound of birds in the clearing, enjoying their obvious delight in being alive. Looking about him, he could see that none of these people had noticed such things, and they would not perceive the goodness in life. Their hearts were set so much upon being busy with "right things" that they had failed to be happy as well. The joy God had intended for man to have was not in them.

"My brothers and sisters, please hear me. I was ordained as an apostle of the Lord Jesus Christ under His own hand. I know something of what he really taught." John paused and walked out among the people in the group. "I was like many of you in that I was very earnest and serious about living the law of God. One time I even suggested to the Lord that fire from heaven be called down on those in a village that did not accept His message. My Lord rebuked me. He told me He had not come to destroy, but to build up; not to hate, but to love. The message of the gospel is a joyful, loving one."

"What about when he was angry with the money lenders in the temple?" shouted a man who had not spoken up before.

John whirled around to answer, and in that split second recognized the trap Satan was working through this man. "I was there," declared John boldly. "Who among you can make the same claim?" None moved or made a sound. More softly now, he went on. "That which you call anger was very carefully done to get attention and disrupt a system that needed to be changed. But there was no negative thought in His heart toward those people, only love. He disliked their actions, but He loved them. While it was true those people were not living and working for salvation the way they should have, they were worthy of being loved. They had lost the true vision of what work and enjoyment really are. The adversary had encouraged them to find false, easy ways to do what naturally is hard. Work is hard, and enjoyment is easy. One tears down, the other builds back up and refreshes. Find ways to enjoy your work, yes, and accept that it is hard. But find time and ways to enjoy the beauties of this world, the wonder in each other's hearts, and laugh together in gratitude, happiness, and joy. The gospel is joy."

John stopped to look at his congregation. Some were listening intently, some had hardened their hearts against his message. He continued, "Those sellers at the temple were committing sin, yes, yet within their hearts the Master still perceived enough good to make the effort to correct them. He had a perfect balance within Him that you have not yet come to understand."

John walked slowly amongst the group now, touching the cheek of a child, patting the shoulder of a woman who was crying. "The message of the Lord is to work hard and enjoy life, just as you need to be tender with your love when mercy is called for and exacting with it when justice is required. Work hard when it is needed, and rejoice as you enjoy the bounty which He has provided for you. One without the other is not the Lord's way. To become perfect as He is, we must grow complete, we must become whole."

The raven nearby called out, bringing John back to the present. He opened his eyes and looked up at the bird. "You're right," he said. "It is time to take care of things here. That was long ago and far away. This is now."

By the time John got back to his room in the boarding house he was cold and tired. Since he was fasting, he took no thought for food but undressed quickly and knelt beside his bed to pray. Afterwards he got into bed and soon fell fast asleep. It was still a long time until tomorrow morning and church, but he planned on getting an early start in preparation. He was full of anticipation, and wanted to be rested and fresh.

Chapter Eleven

Although Jimmy and Marriane insisted that John sit up front in their Volkswagen, he hurriedly got into the small back seat and refused to come out, so they finally gave up. As the threesome rode to church on a beautiful Sunday morning, John looked out the window and enjoyed the passing scenery while the young couple in the front seats shared a teasing banter.

Terrell expected that having his friend John come to church with them would be a treat. While John knew that for some that would be the case, he also knew there would be those who would find his presence disturbing, at best.

"Come to dinner with us after church today," Marriane invited over her shoulder. "We're having my famous fried chicken and German chocolate cake."

"That will be just fine," John answered, "if they don't kick me out of church and threaten your membership for bringing me."

Raising an eyebrow, Jimmy looked into the back seat through his rear view mirror and grinned. "I know a lot rowdier people than you who are allowed in there. But if anyone starts toward you with tar and feathers, I'll let you know so you'll have plenty of time to run."

Jimmy pulled into the parking lot of the LDS chapel which was already quite full of cars and trucks. John had often thought about how much he liked some of the older church buildings with their individual looks and separate personalities, especially those with stained glass in them. But he also thought it was nice how with these new uniform buildings, a person could quickly find a chapel in a strange place by its similarity to others of its kind.

As the three entered the front door, Jimmy and Marriane stopped to talk to another young couple. John followed them in and stood in the foyer looking around. It was easy for the members to recognize that he was a visitor, and a middle-aged man who stood at the chapel door as a "greeter" came up to John and welcomed him. "Hello, my name is Ralph Peterson. Good morning."

"Good morning to you," replied John.

"Are you visiting?" asked the man.

"Yes, I am. I've heard good things about your church and thought I would see for myself."

"Well, you're certainly welcome here. Our Sunday School will start in the chapel in just a few minutes."

Jimmy came over to John and the greeter, and put his arm around the latter's shoulders. "You'd better watch out for this one, Brother Peterson. He looks like a spy from Church headquarters in Salt Lake."

John shook his head at Jimmy. "Actually," said John, "I'm just someone that had the uncertain luck of being befriended by the Larson family."

"Oh, you two know each other? Are you friends with the bishop?" Brother Peterson asked, a little bewildered. Then, his face reddening, he said to John, "I get it, you're really a member and this is a joke on me!"

Before John could say anything to soothe the feelings of the man, Brother Peterson had excused himself none too gracefully and gone back to stand by the door. Every now and then, he would look back at John and Jimmy with an irritated expression.

"I thought you were going to help me stay away from the tar and feathers, not push me into it," said John.

"Oh, these people are a pain," exclaimed Jimmy. "Hardly any of them has any sense of humor. I'm sure glad I didn't serve my mission here. Who would have enjoyed joining these people?" Then he saw Marriane beckoning him from the doorway of the chapel and said to John, "Come on, Sunday School is starting."

The meeting began like most in the LDS church, with prelude music being played. John noticed very few people were listening to it. There seemed to be a general consensus that visiting about personal matters was permissible and even expected before the meeting started. The atmosphere of reverence and respite from the world that could have been there was driven away by the chatter and irreverence of the members. John saw Shirley Larson and her brood over on the other side of the room, and he lifted his hand in salute to them when they saw him. At least they were reverent! Bishop Larson and his counselors were on the stand where they were expected to be. The bishop's face had an annoyed look as he surveyed the congregation.

The opening exercises started with the ward Sunday School president welcoming everyone. It took a while before everyone quieted down, and John wondered if they had really heard what he had to say. There was an opening song followed by a prayer. For a few moments John enjoyed the calm in the room, but it quickly left when the prayer was over. Song practice was mostly remarkable for its lackluster singing and low amount of interest in the direction of the chorister. John looked around him. I know these are basically good-hearted people, he thought. If only they were more open to the Spirit! If only they would let go of all their momentary worldly concerns long enough to accept and feel the peace and joy God offers them.

Later, the start of the Gospel Doctrine class seemed to promise better things. John sat with Terrell and Shirley on one side of him, and the younger adult Larsons on the other. The instructor was enthusiastic and had obviously spent time going over the lesson material. John's optimism, however, starting lagging when discussion began on the "gospel" issues of the lesson.

"So you see," said the instructor, "it takes a lot of discipline to live correctly all the time. From Jesus' teachings, we learn that we have to work very hard at living the gospel or we will fail. I can tell you personally it has been a struggle for me to keep going at times. Why, only yesterday I felt like just sitting by the window and drifting off for a while. I had to pray very hard not to give into the temptation. It is so important not to waste the precious time God has blessed us with."

An elderly woman perked up and said, "It gets even harder when you get older. Enduring to the end is so difficult. It would be so easy to let down sometimes. But I know we are to live our lives by the sweat of our brows. Life is full of hardships, and it requires effort to get through it. Plain and simple."

Turning to look at John, Jimmy shook his head and whispered, "Do you think they were all born old? The next comment out of their mouths should be something about lazy 'young folks.'"

A middle-aged man spoke up and said, "I think that's why the kids of this church are having so many problems. They think life is supposed to be easy. When I was growing up, we expected life to be hard. Playing was something you did when you retired. When you had earned it." Jimmy winked meaningfully at John.

The instructor continued, "What I find hard to accept is, when you tell people they are not living the way they should, they get mad at you. Seems to me a bit of honest criticism does people good, and we should be grateful someone cares enough to show us what's what."

John listened sadly, noting how similar this was to other incidents, including the one he had remembered the day before while he had been out walking. Time goes on, the world spins 'round, and people keep making the same mistakes. It's easier for them to shape the gospel to fit their own misconceptions than it is for them to enlarge themselves to live up to real truth, he thought.

John raised his hand. "Yes?" invited the instructor.

"Excuse me," John said mildly. "I'm not a member of your congregation, but I'd like to say something about all this." Most everyone turned to get a better look at this "new face." From the side of his mouth, Jimmy quipped, "Here come the tar and feathers."

"When I read the New Testament, I see and hear a Savior that taught everything you are talking about." Jimmy turned to look at John with a surprised look. Many of the older folks and some of the younger ones nodded their approval. "I also hear a Jesus that taught happiness and joy. He said He came so we might all have 'life, and have it more abundantly.' Sometimes His message seems to get shifted into a 'worker bee' mentality, where the harder you work, the more righteous you're supposed to be. It seems to me that a balance is what the Lord asks from us. I believe that sometimes those who take the time to play are closer to being a 'child of God' than those who think they need to work their way into heaven. Maybe we need to love to play, as well as to work."

A woman with a pinched face raised her hand and spoke. "I don't want to offend you, but we all know what the gospel says. We aren't like some other churches that teach you to expect the 'universe to provide all your needs, if you but send forth positive vibrations.' This is a church that says to choose righteousness. And that means to work hard at it,"

Terrell Larson was looking at John with a concentration so powerful it could have peeled paint off a barn wall. He felt that as the bishop he needed to find a way to ease through this conflict. Yet he agreed strongly with what John was saying.

John laughed inside himself and said, "I'm far from perfect, and I've struggled not to be judgmental of others who understand differently than I do what it means to be alive and live the gospel. Most of us see part of God's truth, and form the rest out of our own desires. One of my favorite quotes is, 'May we be tolerant of those who choose to sin differently than we do.'

"There was a time I felt I knew exactly what God expected of everyone, and when they didn't do it, I saw it as my duty to set them straight. But I was wrong, and the Lord told me I was wrong." At John's last statement, Terrell's eyes widened.

"The message of the gospel is a joyful, loving one," John said softly. The room had become very quiet. Many were experiencing the touch of the Spirit of God more powerfully than they ever had before. "The Lord loves and cares for all his children. As they work to be obedient and fulfill their measure of creation they are able to be more fully blessed. He wants us to work to find joy, strange as that may seem at first."

John went on to say much the same as what he remembered saying to another congregation so long ago. Unfortunately, the response was also much the same.

* * *

The rest of the Gospel Doctrine class had been mostly filler after what John had said. Everyone seemed to want to drop the discussion and go on with other things. And John didn't feel prompted to speak again. The sacrament meeting talks later were, interestingly enough, on how following the Savior means to grow in many different ways.

Some of the members looked over at John when the speaker, who had not been present for the Gospel Doctrine class, was urging greater gratitude for blessings received, and rejoicing for the good in life.

The ride home from church was much quieter than the one on the way to it. Marriane and Jimmy were deep in their own thoughts, and John seemed to have used up all the words he had left in him. Jimmy was about to say something when a battered-looking station wagon started to pass them and then drove alongside instead. To Jimmy's horror, the driver began to edge his car against the little bug as he honked his horn and made obscene gestures at the three occupants.

"Who the heck is that?" yelled Jimmy. But John had immediately recognized Jake Skoggins as the other driver. Jake had been driving by the church when he noticed Jimmy's car as it had pulled out of the church parking lot. The fact that Jake saw John in the car as well with this group of "stinkin' Mormons" justified his giving them a little scare.

As the larger car made contact with the smaller, Jimmy strained to keep from losing control of his little car. The right wheels of the bug lurched onto the narrow shoulder of the country road, immediately losing traction in the icy gravel. The bug fishtailed, then shot over the shoulder and flew off the road, hurtling toward a huge tree. The last thing Jake heard as he sped away was Marriane's scream.

Jake hadn't counted on actually running them off the road. He had just had a little joke in mind, but the little car had shoved over a lot easier than he had counted on. "What did their car have to do that for?" he muttered as he drove quickly away.

Chapter Twelve

The resulting crash from Jake Skoggins's practical joke put Jimmy's pregnant wife, Marriane, in the hospital for a few days although Jimmy and John had sustained only a few cuts and bruises from the ordeal. Now, two days after the crash, as John swept up the grain that had leaked out of some feed bags onto the loading dock, he could see Jimmy's bug sitting behind the last feed bin. It had a large dent in the front and a shattered windshield where it had partially wrapped around a tree. John looked up to see Terrell drive into the yard and jump out of his truck. "How's Marriane doing?" John called out as Terrell came over.

Terrell's face clouded momentarily, then eased. "Well, she's okay right now, but we were sure worried for awhile. Jimmy brought her home from the hospital this morning, and he and I gave her a blessing." His face tightened up again before he sighed and said, "Oh well, the Lord is watching over her and the baby. I'll just have to leave it in His hands."

"Things are going to work out the way they need to," John comforted Terrell. "You're right, there's nothing we can do by worrying about it."

Both men stood silently for a few moments, neither in a hurry to move on to something else. Terrell spoke at last, quietly and more to himself than to John. "How could someone do a thing like that, anyway? What's wrong with people anymore? You know, I talked to the sheriff, and he told me Jake Skoggins only got a misdemeanor charge out of what he did to Seth Templeman." Terrell's face grew darker as he talked. "I really have a hard time accepting that someone who was just arrested for assault is already out on the streets. And now, no one's seen him since Sunday. I hope they find him for what he's done now." John could see that Terrell was full of anger. "What happened to law? What happened to justice?"

Sensing the downward change of heart going on in his friend, John reached out to Terrell. "The Lord heals those who suffer at the hands of the wicked. He will settle with the wicked in His own time and in His own way, though it may not come as soon as we would like it to. There has always been good and evil in this world. Evil can't leave good alone. The saddest part is, when evil is done, it hurts those who do it more than those they do it to. The negative thoughts and actions twist them in horrible ways."

Terrell had been listening, and now he thought, By their fruits ye shall know them. The thought took him far into himself, where he came across another thought that had been very important but forgotten until that moment. His focus shifted back outside of himself, and he fixed his gaze upon John. "That reminds me, I have a few questions for you. What you said to Matt on Thanksgiving got me to thinking. You don't mind if I get to know you better, do you?" asked Terrell with a grin, having much the same look a cat gets when it thinks it has the mouse cornered.

John did not appear concerned with Terrell's investigation of him. He took the broom he had been leaning on and began to sweep again. "Don't mind a bit. I'll give it all the attention and interest it deserves." Then he swept quickly across the dock and down the steps toward the feed bins with Terrell in hot pursuit.

"Now wait a minute," called Terrell. "I'm supposed to be the boss here, at least when Teresa isn't around." He glanced quickly toward the office door and turned to find John was already ten feet up the ladder on the outside of the first feed bin.

"John, you come back down here," hollered Terrell. "I want to talk to you."

John stopped climbing but he didn't come back down. He looked down and said, "Are you ordering me as my boss, or are you asking as my friend?"

Terrell squirmed a bit with that, then said more calmly, "I don't have the right to ask as the boss, and I probably wouldn't as the friend. So how about I ask as an LDS bishop?" Terrell was pretty pleased with himself over that bit of mental dancing around. He grinned as he stood looking up, thinking he had finally gotten John where he wanted him.

John nodded slowly, saying, "Well, that makes all the difference in the world. The only possible thing I can say to that is, Sorry, Bishop, but I've got work to do." And with that, John quickly climbed the ladder and disappeared into the top of the bin.

Terrell's smile evaporated. He jumped up on the ladder, calling, "Wai . . . Wait a minute. All I want to do is ask you a few questions." However, in his haste, Terrell slipped off the ladder and fell the five feet to the ground, banging his right shin on the bottom rung. "Ow!" he yelped. "John, come back," pleaded Terrell as he began to climb up the ladder, more slowly this time. His leg was killing him, and he stopped every other step to rub it and grimace over his troubles. "All I wanted to do was talk a little bit," he moaned to himself.

John, meanwhile, was chuckling to himself as he checked the feed for any sign of moisture that might have leaked in from the roof. He was also looking for bird or rodent activity that so often made havoc of the feed storage. It wasn't in his nature to be deceptive, but this wasn't the time to get into a detailed discussion with anyone about who he was. Still, he had to admit Terrell was making the funniest racket climbing and complaining all the way up the ladder.

"All I wanted to do was ask a few small questions. What's the big deal?" asked Terrell as he finally hauled himself to the top of the ladder. Stepping inside the bin, he opened his mouth to talk to John and found . . . no one! "Where in the . . . ?" he said to no one. There was no sign of John in the feed bin, and there was no place he could have hidden; Terrell was baffled. Shaking his head in amazement, he turned to look out the doorway of the bin and almost fell the twenty feet to the ground. There at the far end of the loading dock, walking down the steps to go around front of the building, was John. "How did he do that?" exclaimed Terrell.

Now Terrell was a determined man in anyone's book, but all this disappearing business was weakening his resolve. Still, he had just about made up his mind to try one last time to talk to John when the loudspeaker called him to come up front to the store. Shaking his head, Terrell accepted that he would have to let go. Maybe another time would be better for getting to know the real John.

* * *

Around five o'clock that afternoon, Teresa was putting away her work and tidying up the office before leaving. She was extremely pleased with herself and proud she had finally nailed down where that lost shipment of feed had gone to. Sure, when you can figure it out and ask the farmers if they got an extra shipment they'll tell you, she thought, but do they volunteer the information? No way! They figure—conveniently for them—that if you don't ask then it's just a gift for their "good business." I have to watch those guys like a hawk!

The door opened and she looked up to see John, who had come in to look over the orders for tomorrow's deliveries. "So what've you got going tonight, Teresa? You going to the Single Adult get-together at the stake center in Clayton City tonight?" He grinned innocently at her.

Teresa had, well, she had gotten used to him—sort of. At least she had accepted that he was going to be around for a while, so it was no use making a big deal about it. On the other hand, she had no intention of becoming too friendly with him. He was a friend to her father and the rest of the family, but as far as she was concerned, he was just an employee here. That meant they would have a positive working relationship, nothing else.

"Yes, I'm planning to attend this evening," she said curtly. "But I'm sure you have more exciting things to do."

"Actually, I'm interested in going myself. Something tells me I could get a lot of good out of it." said John with a twinkle in his eyes that belied the serious expression on his face.

Teresa had an inkling that John was fishing for an invitation, or at the very least a ride, but she had no intention of sharing the forty-minute ride with him each way.

"Well, I'm sure my father can line you up a ride if you want to go," she replied as she turned to finish her end of the day's routine and end this unsettling conversation.

"As a matter of fact, he did suggest someone I could ride with. He said he was sure they would be happy to do it."

Teresa felt like she had been let off the hook. She could afford to be nice now. Breathing a sigh of relief, she turned back to John. "I'm sure someone will be happy to give you a ride. Especially when my father recommended them to you!" She meant it sincerely, now that she knew she was off the hook. Actually John was nice—even though he was also aggravating!

"I'm glad you feel that way, Teresa," John smiled, "since it was you he said would give me a ride tonight." Teresa's knees went weak, and her shock was quickly replaced with anger.

"He said I would take you!? I . . . I was planning on . . ." she sputtered, finally managing a sarcastic "Did he also happen to say what time I would be by to pick you up?"

Ignoring her sarcasm, John scratched his head absently. "I think about seven o'clock is what he said." He came over to her and took her hand. "I can't tell you how grateful I am for your generosity. You have a remarkable charity for others."

Teresa stood open-mouthed in shock and disbelief, too stunned to reply, so John let go of her hand and said goodbye. "Well, I guess I'll see you later. I live on Faron Street at the Ballshide boarding house. I'll watch for you. Thanks again." Then he was out the door, leaving Teresa stunned and wondering what had happened to her careful plans against letting this man into her life. Muttering to herself in frustration, she picked up her purse, stomped out the office door, and slammed it behind her.

Chapter Thirteen

After picking up John, it had been a long, quiet drive from the Ballshide boardinghouse to the Clayton City Stake Center. The same uneasy feelings she had struggled with since their talk that night came back as they sat only inches apart. Part of her longed to open herself up to him while part of her wished to flee and never see him again. She wondered what it was about him that got her all jumbled up inside. She had been doing just fine before he came around, and now . . . now, it was all harder somehow. What she had thought was clear and straightforward didn't make as much sense to her as it did before. Life had been simpler, more defined before John had shown up at their house.

Afraid John would once again speak to her with words and tenderness that she had no way to combat, Teresa sat still in her own silence, behind layer after layer of tense and careful camouflage. He had the power to reach deep into her soul, as he had before. She worried what it might do this time. He had tried to make conversation with her several times, but her replies had been short. The sound of air rushing past the moving car in the darkness was the only noise. John gave himself to the moment and found peace while Teresa kept grinding away on the question of finding someone else he could ride back with.

When they arrived, she quickly excused herself to go talk with someone else—anyone else! John knew no one, but he enjoyed watching people. As he watched he would occasionally smile to himself, as if he knew someone intimately.

The speaker that evening was interesting, if a little predictable. His basic point was that the more cheerful you were, the better chance you had for being liked by those around you. His own social life, he admitted, was not as yet all that wonderful, but he knew this way would eventually bear good fruit. Those who listened generally nodded yes, and wondered "Okay, now what?"

As people filed out of the chapel to enter the multi-purpose room for the dance, Teresa made several inquiries about finding John another ride home. Each of those she talked to had a reason for not being able to help. The more she asked, the more irritated she became, until her only desire was to leave and go home. She didn't even care if she had to drive John back as long as she could leave right then. The whole evening had taken on a nightmarish quality.

When John asked with complete innocence, "Why do you want to go home when the fun is just starting?" it was all she could do to maintain her sense of dignity and bearing, and not just walk out, leaving John to find his own way home.

"I just want to, that's all," she insisted. "I'm not feeling well." It wasn't really a lie, she told herself. She really did feel miserable.

"Well," John said amiably, "if you ask me—"

"But I didn't ask you!" Teresa shot back.

"—you'd feel better if you just loosened up," John suggested softly.

Teresa's sense of frustration reached its full level, and ignited. Confused and overwhelmed, she was sure of only one thing: she didn't need anyone to tell her how to live her life!

"You can find your own way home, for all I care. I don't care what my father thinks!" She turned on her heel and marched out of the gym, down the hall and out the door of the stake center, sparks of indignation flying as she stomped off.

If Teresa could have gone out to her car, got in, and drove away, it would have been fine. She would have had the last word, and could have given him a smug, "I showed you" look when he came into the office on Monday.

Things didn't work out that way. Teresa got into her car all right, but found it wouldn't start. She tried everything she could think of but to no avail. The dreams of comeuppance on John she had been savoring just moments before faded away. Slamming her hands down on the steering wheel, she sat looking into space and fuming. After a few moments, she tried the ignition once more before finally admitting that the car was not going to start for her.

Overcome by the reality of the situation, unable to run, she burst into tears. What a horrible night! It was the worst night of her life! How did these things happen to her? Why did these things happen to her?!

It was bad enough that her father had wrangled her into this whole situation. The drive from Crystal had been stressful beyond words. Being around John upset Teresa in ways she didn't understand. Whenever she was around him, it was as if he knew her thoughts and could unlock within her the places she had never unlocked for anyone and see past all the pretense. She felt almost naked under his gaze, although there was nothing of lust or anything unclean in his look. And she could not stand to be bared to anyone that way. Her only defense was to avoid him.

She realized that the other members of the family all seemed to get along with John. She had watched them with him, had seen their unhesitating acceptance of him. She had noticed how gentle and kind he was, especially with little Amanda and her two rambunctious brothers. He put up with their stupid practical jokes, even finding time to help them with various school projects or scout activities—things they would normally ask their father for help with. But Dad wasn't always available, now that he had a bishop's duties. John didn't seem to mind helping out with the family. In fact, he acted as if he were honored that they asked him. And that was another thing: didn't her father care that John was taking over his fatherly role? Even Amanda had taken to crawling into John's arms and asking him to read to her, a practice she had formerly reserved only for her father.

John seemed kind, really, but he wasn't a member of the family. So what exactly did he want from them? What was he getting out of it? It was all very confusing, and no one seemed to understand what Teresa was upset about. She wished John had never come into their lives. She wished her parents could see what John was doing to them all. She had tried to talk to her mother after the incident at church, when John had spoken in Sunday School and made them all look like fools. She had been mortified. He wasn't even a member, for heaven's sake, and her father had just sat like a lump of clay and let John spout off like that! She had told her mother there were people in the ward who avoided them now because of it, who were watching the Larsons now and wondering just what was going on, but her mother had not seemed to understand or take it seriously. She patted Teresa on the shoulder as if she were a child and said, "Teresa, there will always be people who make judgments against you for what they don't understand. Don't let it worry you."

Don't let it worry you! Teresa had wanted to cry out. How could it not? People would begin to question her father's ability as a bishop; some people were already whispering about her behind her back. Of course it mattered what people thought. Hadn't her parents always told her to live so that others would think well of her?

Teresa sat, still clenching the steering wheel, sobbing quietly a while longer at the frustrating, out-of-control mess that had become her life. Then, drying her eyes, she pulled herself back together. I'll just ask someone inside to help me, she decided.

The dance was in full swing when Teresa walked back into the gym. She surveyed the crowd and finally found someone she knew was experienced in auto mechanics. Threading her way through the dancing couples, she came up to and tapped a tall, blonde fellow on the shoulder. "Ted," she asked, "can you take a moment and look at my car? I can't get it to start."

Forty minutes later, it seemed that the majority of the male participants at the dance were congregated around Teresa's car. Everyone had a theory about why it wouldn't start, but no one was able to get it up and running. Grease and oil marked most hands and arms, plus a few faces. They all seemed to be having a good time, but the car still wasn't going anywhere.

Teresa was standing in the doorway of the building with a few other young women. "Wouldn't you think with all of them out there someone would have figured out what the problem is?" one girl laughed, although the girls were none too pleased that the time that they could have spent with the young men was being taken over by a car!

And where is John? thought Teresa. At least he could offer to help.

* * *

John was many miles away from Teresa and her car problems. He had left the stake center shortly after Teresa's march out to her car and hitched a ride into town with a passing motorist. At the moment, he was walking along a street in one of the seedier parts of town. He didn't know exactly what he was looking for, but he knew he would recognize the place when he saw it. He opened himself up to inspiration, and after a few blocks, a sign caught his eye hanging over the sidewalk: "Wild Man Video."

John stood a moment, peering through the dirty windows. He saw videos for rent, arcade machines, and pool tables. Across the room was a makeshift bar and grill. It felt dirty and cheap; the place obviously was not one of the city's finer establishments.

A certainty came to his mind, and a warmth to his heart. This is it, thought John, he's here. He pushed open the door and walked in.

The first thing that met John was the smell of the place. An odor like cigarettes, musty sweat, grease, and cheap cologne. The heavy, balding man behind the counter turned as John came through the door. Looking John over carefully, he figured John was no problem and went back to his newspaper and cigarette. The teenage boys at the arcade video games didn't bother to turn from their quarter-fed adventures at the sound of a new arrival, but the pool players squinted at John from underneath the bright lights over the tables.

John must not have looked all that interesting, because a moment later he was forgotten. This suited him fine, since he knew the person he was looking for was there; he wasn't sure exactly where. Being ignored allowed John to wander around and casually check everyone out.

There was quite a pool game going on at the table in the corner, with a sizable stack of money in bets piled on one of the side rails where everyone could keep an eye on it. One of the players was a large hulk of a boy, with a high school football letterman's jacket on. He had a cue stick in his left hand, and was leaning over the pool table eyeballing the layout of the balls. Two other boys sat on the scarred-up stools against the wall, making comments to their friend in the jacket.

John watched the three for a while until he was sure the person he sought was not among them. Walking over to a vacant stool a little way off from the game, he sat down and looked around. He's here somewhere, thought John. I can feel it. Then he saw the lone figure leaning back against the corner. He was much smaller than the other three and seemed, well . . . careful. Or maybe "wary" was a better description. Seeing Nathan Morse for the first time, John knew that behind his cool, street-wise manner was a frightened young boy.

"So are you going to shoot, or are you expecting the balls to fall in because they're getting tired?" Nathan now spoke to the other player, who didn't even bother to look up.

"Watch your mouth, punk!" replied the football player casually as he rose from the table. "It don't make any difference if I beat you quick, or I beat you slow. Either way the money is mine." He leaned forward and rammed his pool stick at the cue ball. The object of his intense concentration, the four ball, was met by the charging cue ball and flew toward the far corner pocket. With a loud bang the ball disappeared into the pocket as the football jock rose up and smiled in Nathan's direction. "Consider your money gone," he gloated.

"It ain't over 'til it's over, Horace," was Nathan's studiously cool reply.

Horace Wheatley, known to his friends and school sports circles, if not his parents, as "Buff," didn't take kindly to anyone using his real name. He might have to put up with it at home, but he didn't here. He liked being compared to a buffalo, and this nobody was going to pay for his smart mouth.

Buff slammed his stick down on the table and took a few menacing steps toward Nathan. At the same time, his pals slid off their stools in anticipation of a fight. But Nathan had anticipated Buff's anger; in fact, he had counted on it. It was obvious to him that he was very close to losing all his money on this game. After struggling to scrape it together, he certainly didn't want to lose it to this dinosaur.

With all the money he had on the line, and going hungry a real possibility, Nathan calculated he needed to upset Buff's run of successful shots before it was too late. Sure, he knew how easy it was to get out of hand when you're dealing with "cave men," but this was a desperate situation. Nathan had felt it was worth the gamble. Now he wasn't so sure.

As Buff came forward, Nathan instinctively raised his own cue stick until it was aimed right at Buff's groin. He was no match for Buff's strength, so his only chance was to get in the first shot.

John watched all this carefully, considering what needed to be done. He thought briefly how much Nathan was like his father, Harry, in his ability to get into trouble quickly. To onlookers, it seemed like John just "appeared" at the side of the pool table and carelessly began to rifle through the money. "Sure is a lot of money riding on this game," he said in a deliberately loud voice.

The word "money" triggered something in Buff's mind and he lurched to a stop from his intended attack on Nathan. Whirling around, he spied John standing beside the table, holding the money in his hands. "Put it down." bellowed Buff. His interest in teaching Nathan a lesson was temporarily forgotten, replaced by this new threat.

John appeared as calm as a butterfly on a stone in a pasture. He didn't seem concerned that a beefy, red-faced bully was now standing only arm's length away from him. Of course, it had been his intention to shift the focus from Nathan to himself, but looking at the difference in sizes between Buff and John, one had to wonder how things were going to turn out.

John put the money back on the edge of the pool table, leaving one hand on it. "It's a lot of money on such a game." He smiled at Buff calmly.

Buff took a half step forward, glaring at John, who stood quietly with an air of confidence. Buff didn't like how this guy felt to him. He looked older, but so what? Buff had licked plenty of the college guys who came to work on the farms around Clayton City in the summer. No, it wasn't age or size that bothered Buff; this guy was about his same height, but slighter, without the bulk. What was unsettling to him was John's calm, unfrightened gaze. Buff had learned early on in his life that whether you beat someone or they beat you actually was determined inside. Before there was ever a punch thrown, the battle was fought between your eyes and the other guy's. If you thought you could whip him, really thought it, then it happened. The look in

John's eyes said it all.

Now Buff had a problem. He quickly considered his options. He really wanted that money, so he had to figure some way to work this all out. Mustering his coolest look, he said, "When I get through playing the shrimp here, you can be next."

"Sounds good to me," said John, walking over to sit on one of the stools by the wall. The immediate danger to Nathan was now past, so John was content to wait and watch what would happen next.

Buff turned back to the table and picked up his pool cue. "This is it," he challenged, "the last shot of the night. Kiss your money goodbye!" He stroked a smooth bank shot with the cue ball that kissed his last ball into the pocket. "All right, ALL RIGHT!" exulted Buff.

Nathan did not move from the corner. All he saw was John, and all he thought was how his plan to mess up Buff's concentration had been stopped by this guy from nowhere. What business was it of his, anyway?

Buff slapped his cue stick down on the table and turned toward Nathan again. "Now I finish teaching you to watch your mouth. Street scum like you need to know their place!"

"My turn," said John as he slid off his stool. He casually walked right in front of Buff on his way to the cue stick rack. Selecting one, he held it up to his eye and sighting down it he said to himself, "It will have to do." Then he walked back to the pool table and ran his hand over the surface, feeling its varying ridges and valleys. Buff had turned to watch all this with a suspicious eye, his euphoria and bravado of the previous moment quickly fading away. Maybe this guy was even more trouble than he had thought. Still, the name of the game was to follow through on his challenge.

"Soon as I get through with him," said Buff as he motioned toward Nathan, "then you can show us how bad we play around here." His final words dripped sarcasm.

"I don't really expect that it will be much of a game, but I've got things to do, so it'll have to do for now. That is, if you aren't backing out." John nonchalantly picked up the cue ball and placed it near a place on the table as though he had done this many times before.

"Okay, hot shot, how much money are you backing up your big talk with?" shot back Buff.

John gently stroked his stick forward and tapped the cue ball down the table, where it softly bounced off of the cushion and came back toward him. "I don't gamble, so we have to find something else to make this game interesting."

Buff snorted. "So what's the point of even bothering with you? You lose and I waste my time!"

The cue ball John had hit had slowly been coming closer to the cushion next to him on his end of the table. As Buff was speaking, the cue ball came to a rest exactly against the table cushion. The mark of extremely good control in a pool player, it was usually the sign to designate who started the game by breaking the rack of balls.

"Maybe we could make it interesting anyway," said John quietly as he continued to survey the table. "If I win, the kid in the corner and I leave without any trouble. If you win, well, then . . . I'll hold your jacket while you punch his lights out!"

Nathan came alive in the corner on that last part of John's comments. "What the he . . .?" he swore.

Buff laughed, "I can take this little jerk with or without your help." He looked over at his buddies who were smiling like jackals in anticipation of a little bloodletting.

"I don't need your help," muttered Nathan, but no one was paying any attention to him.

"Sure, I figure if I lose, you could always go ahead and pound on him, but . . . I won't lose. After watching you play, I'm sure of that." John's smile said, So how about it? Are you man enough to try it, or are you going to turn and run?

Buff glared at John. Then he looked at Nathan and his buddies. He had the money, he didn't need another game. But pride always demands more payments, and to Buff image was everything. He couldn't walk away from anything that might damage his reputation—not with anyone watching, that is. "Rack 'em up!" he growled.

One of Buff's friends jumped off his stool and racked up the pool balls. When everything was set, Buff motioned John to go first. "You're going to need it," he laughed.

John positioned himself and the cue ball to break the balls at the other end of the table. He stood with a faraway look on his face for a moment as if he were listening for something. Then he leaned over the table and carefully sighted down his stick at the cue ball.

John's stroke was sure and straight. The cue ball shot away and struck the front pool ball in the triangular formation slightly to the left of straight on. What happened next was hard to believe. Even after it was over no one moved for a few seconds. Buff, his buddies, and Nathan had seen all fifteen of the pool balls explode from their racked formation. Every pocket on the table received at least one ball, and most more. Except for the cue ball that rolled lazily back toward where it had started, the table was completely empty.

"Guess that means I win, huh?" mused John. "So, looks like the kid and I'll be going now. See you around sometime."

Buff had been blown away by John's shot, but he had no intention of letting these two get away. Both of these guys had poked holes in his ego tonight, and he knew that the best way to fix things was to wipe the floor with them. His buddies had read the situation the same way and were now standing behind John, waiting for the signal to start.

Funny though, at that exact moment a Clayton City police officer came through the door of the place. He had been on his way home after his shift and for some reason decided to stop in and rent some videos to watch that night with his wife. "Hi, Mike," he called to the old man back of the counter. "Got any new ones for me to look at tonight? I was driving by and something said to stop in and look at what you got."

At the sight of the police officer, Buff and his friends tried to look like they were just having a friendly pool game. John quickly grabbed Nathan by the arm in a vise-like grip and headed for the door before the would-be assailants noticed. Caught off guard, Nathan didn't realize what was happening until they were out the door. "What the . . . ?"

John looked back through the door at Buff, who was trying to look casual while at the same time hurrying after them. John and Nathan took off down the darkened street.

Chapter Fourteen

Nathan gasped for air in great gulps. As he leaned hard against a brick wall, his head swam and his stomach churned. Everything was forgotten but the need to rest from the long, tortuous running of the last thirty minutes. The three guys from the pool hall had been hard to shake. If they had caught him, Nathan knew he would have been hurting a lot more than he was now. Yeah, if it weren't for this guy here who had helped him, he wouldn't even be . . .

Nathan painfully raised his head to look for John. The alley they had run down, with its rotting vegetables and assorted booze bottles and trash, was still there. He could even make out through his oxygen-debt haze the trash cans he had run into and sent flying all over the alley. Nathan had been afraid that the noise would alert those that followed them to their position. But there was no sign of three guys or even of the guy who helped him out of the jam back at Wild Man's.

Nathan finally got his breathing to slow down. His heart didn't feel like it was going to jump right out of his chest anymore, and it seemed like he was going to survive after all. Carefully he made his way back to the street. Stepping out onto the pavement, he caught a bit of movement out of the corner of his right eye. It was the stranger who had helped him.

"We're okay now. I doubled back while you were resting and made sure we lost them," he said now.

Nathan was glad to be rid of those jerks at the pool hall, and he might even have admitted John had been some help. But, before anything else went on, he wanted to know what this guy's angle was, 'cause no one ever did anything for nothing!

"Let me guess," spoke up John. "You want to know who I am, and why I bothered to help you, right? Since I can see by the look on your face that I got that right, I'll just jump right in with both feet. My name is John, and I'm, well, let me put it some way that will make sense to you. Do you remember that TV show a few years back about the guy who was an angel, and went around helping people?"

"Yeah, so what?" asked Nathan.

"Well, that's like me. I get a kick from going around and helping people. That's pretty easy, right?"

"So you're like an angel. Sure, and I'm the Easter Bunny!" Nathan shook his head and spit onto the street. "What are you really? A cop? 'Cause if you are, I don't know anything about what Jimmy Bilton did with that stuff he heisted from Emery Electronics last week."

"Oh, that's easy," replied John. "Jimmy stashed it under the '65 Chevy in the junkyard where you used to hide all your things. He figured if anyone found it, they would also find your old wallet in there and think you stole the stuff."

"Why, that slime . . . !" Nathan started to exclaim and then stopped. How did this guy know all about where he had stashed stolen stuff in the past, or how that rat Jimmy had set him up? Nathan looked at John even more suspiciously now. He wanted to ask how John knew all this, but that wouldn't be cool.

John added, "Of course, if the police knew about the stereo you heisted out of that Camero over on Miller Street, they would probably be a bit upset."

That was it. That was the part that tipped Nathan over and out of his "I'm too cool to be surprised by anything" masquerade. Now he literally exploded. "How did you know that?" he yelled, glaring at John.

John smiled, pointed at himself with both thumbs up, and said matter of factly, "I told you, I'm like that angel guy on TV."

"You're nuts!" said Nathan and began walking quickly away from John. He had not gone very far before he again had company.

I don't care, thought Nathan, he can do what he wants. Forget it! I'm out of here. This guy is too weird!

A police car prowled around the corner and slowed as it drew near John and Nathan. The car began to pace behind them as they walked along, so John turned and waved at the police officer. Nathan, meantime, was trying to disappear inside of his jacket.

"Evening, officer," said John as he walked over to the police car. The officer rolled down his window to look them over and evaluate if there was anything odd about their walking down the street at this time of night. John looked up in the sky and said, "Sure is a nice night. There must be a million stars up there."

"Where you boys headed?" asked the officer. He didn't see anything in John, but something about Nathan seemed familiar to him.

"We were heading out to, ah, the church," John said. "There's a dance going on there, and we thought we might just drop in and take a look at it."

"There aren't any churches around here," said the officer with a frown.

"It's out of town a ways. You know the Mormon church out on Sasson road? That's where we're heading."

The officer chewed on a toothpick before asking Nathan, "So you're going to a church dance?"

Nathan had said not too long ago he would rather be in jail than go to church ever again. At the moment, though, that didn't seem like such a good attitude. The longer that cop kept looking at him, the greater the chance he would remember the time he had almost caught Nathan ripping off tools from the gas station on 8th and Henry. Nathan had almost lost his lunch when the guy had come cruising down the alley. What dumb luck!

"Uh, yeah. That's where we was going, out to the dance. Best time around!" After Nathan said it he pretended to have something in his eye and turned away, covering his face.

The officer chewed on the toothpick a little more and said, "Okay, have a good time." He quickly drove away as John watched the glow of the patrol car's tail lights fade into the darkness.

"Nice guy, that one. Hope he remembers to get something for his wife's birthday tomorrow!" Turning around, he found himself alone and talking to no one; Nathan had already split.

When John caught up with him he said, "What about the dance at the stake center?"

Nathan muttered, "Man, you are crazy! I'm not going to no dance, especially a Mormon dance. So get lost!"

"Yeah, but—"

"Look, I'm not Mormon and I don't go to church anyway," Nathan shot back. "I wouldn't do it for my folks, and I don't have to do it for you. I mean, I don't even know you. Thanks for savin' my bacon and all that, but who asked you? So get out of my life!"

As Nathan talked, a car came slowly down the street and pulled over in front of them. The driver got out and called, "John?"

"Hey, Suzie!" said John with a big smile. "Funny meeting you here."

Suzie was a bubbly, perky seventeen-year-old. She was president of her seminary class, student body president, and an honor student. She was one of the most popular girls in town, but most of all Suzie loved life and people. She had met John at the grain mill where her friend, Cindy, worked.

"Do you need a ride?" Suzie gave John a hug in greeting. "You're a long way from home."

John put his hand out to take hold of Nathan and replied, "As a matter of fact, we sure could use a ride. We were on our way out to the stake center, but you know how far that is, and how tired we must be already, huh?"

Nathan had been listening and watching all this with quiet interest. He had no desire to go anywhere with John, but Suzie was another matter. She now turned and smiled at him, and his heart flipped over and dribbled all over the street.

"So, who's your friend?" asked Suzie.

"This is Nathan Morse," introduced John. "He and I have been friends for oh, quite a while now."

"Hi," Suzie gave Nathan a dazzling smile. "Any friend of John's must be someone special. I'll be glad to give you a lift." Nathan was so befuddled he couldn't speak. Wherever she wanted him to go, it was all right with him! Nathan might be street smart, but he was a pushover for a smile from a pretty girl.

"Pile in, you two, and we'll be off. My dad let me borrow his car to attend a regional student body president meeting, but he won't anymore unless I get it home before too late!"

Nathan still did not intend to go anywhere with John, but at least he could ride along for a while with this really great looking girl. He would figure out later what to do about this John character.

* * *

When Suzie, John, and Nathan pulled into the stake center parking lot, there were only two guys still looking at Teresa's car. John excused himself from Suzie and left Nathan in her care, since Nathan had practically forgotten John was alive. He went into the stake center and found Teresa, who by this time was exhausted. What little small talk ability she had ever possessed was drained.

"So where have you been?" she asked, although she was too tired to care all that much.

John sidestepped her question, asking one of his own instead. "Weren't you going to leave earlier?"

Teresa flashed a glare at him and admitted unhappily, "My car won't start, so it's a bit hard to drive it anywhere. No one seems to know what's wrong."

"Why don't I take a look at it?" was all he said before turning to go back outside. Teresa nearly had to run to keep up with him, but this was something she was not going to miss for anything. After every guy at the dance had tried and failed to get the car started, there was no way John could possibly do it.

John walked up to Teresa's car. He bent his head and prayed silently, then slipped into the car. "I'm going to try to start it now, so everyone get their hands clear," he called out. A quick turn of the key in the ignition brought the car roaring to life.

Teresa was dumbfounded. In fact, she was so amazed she couldn't say anything at all. And Teresa wasn't the only one; the two guys who had still been working on the car stood with their mouths hanging open. John got out of the car and said to Teresa, "You shouldn't have any more trouble with it tonight, but I'd have somebody take a look at it tomorrow. Oh, and you don't need to give me a ride home after all; someone I know is giving me a lift."

John turned and got into a car with some people Teresa didn't know. She felt empty; there wasn't even enough emotion left inside to feel angry. She drove home in silence.

Chapter Fifteen

About the same time John was bringing Teresa Larson's car back to life, Jake Skoggins sat on a wooden crate that served as one of only two places to sit in the run-down old shack he called home. The house was the only thing he had inherited from his parents. Since their death, Jake had lived in it alone. It had never been much, but had become considerably more dilapidated and ill cared for, now that the upkeep depended on Jake alone. Even as a child he had not been interested in taking care of things.

Now he was hiding out in it, after having slept in his car for several nights. He had been too afraid to come here, knowing that the sheriff would be looking for him after the accident at the Mormon church. Today he had heard about the Larson girl in the hospital. Things just kept getting worse.

Growing up, Jake had been rebellious and headstrong. His father had applied frequent beatings with a strap, hoping to break the negative streak in his son, but to no avail. The bigger Jake had become, the harder it had been for his father to physically discipline him, and gradually his parents had simply withdrawn from him. After that, the schools and the police had been the only structure in Jake's out-of-control life.

When a violent traffic accident had claimed the lives of Jake's parents one night four years ago, the light in his heart dimmed even

more. For despite his seeming lack of interest in family affairs, and
even though his main contact with them consisted almost uniquely of
attempts to leech money, Jake had somehow felt that his parents had
been a doorway he could have opened if he had wanted to. They represented safety and stability—a sameness in his life that gave him a
security base of sorts, weak as it was. At least some kind of goodness
was around, even if he had no use for it at the moment. The deaths of
the only two people in the world that cared anything at all for him had
shut the door on his heart.

Jake looked around him at what had once been a kitchen area. The
place was littered with leftover junk food wrappers, beer bottles, and
broken furniture—the result of the times he had come home drunk
and irritable. During those times his only release had been to take out
his rage at the life he could not control on what little furnishings there
were. The past year, Jake had only used the shack as a place to crawl
back to when his gambling and drinking money ran out. His friends,
if you could call them that, provided him with a place to flop much
of the time. In reality, the few people that hung around with him used
Jake as someone to fight the battles they were too frightened to fight
themselves. Like Willie, the fellow at the tavern when John had cut
Jake short, they had no loyalty nor affection for Jake. Should he
really need their help, he would find himself all alone in the world.

The kindness John had shown Jake, in the face of Jake's violent
attacks, had confused and frightened him. It shook his belief system
of "Do it to them, before they do it to you." His mask of strength and
bravado, which until lately had been successful in giving him a
twisted form of power, didn't work with John. John's actions had upset
Jake's world, and forced him to look inside himself; and what he saw
was unsettling.

Life had always been adversarial for Jake. As a child, he had liked
to have things the way he wanted them, when he wanted them. Being
so much bigger than most of the other kids, it hadn't taken him long
to figure out how he could get his own way.

Jake's father had worked for a manufacturing plant all of his life;
he had never distinguished himself, had never got very far. The small
family—just Jake and his parents—had had enough to care for themselves, but for Jake, that little wasn't enough. As he grew older, and

larger, he wanted more.

He wanted people to look up to him, to respect him. And if he couldn't get respect from them, well, he found that fear was just as good. He liked the way other kids got out of his way. As he grew to manhood physically, he liked the way men got out of his way, too. Often even older, better educated, wealthier men. He felt like he was somebody.

At the warehouse where he worked, he had been given his own section to work, running merchandise from loading dock to storage with the forklift. Nobody bothered him; and Jake, while not overly bright, was a good worker with what he knew. Especially if there was no one else around. So people at work left him alone, and he liked it, thinking it made him special. He liked to boast at the bars that he was a real man, one that could handle the work on his own. He didn't need anybody else's help.

Jake lived in a world of his own. He was on top of it, no matter how small. He had made up a myth of his own invulnerability, and then forgot that he, himself, had created the pretense, convincing himself it was real. John had come along and seen inside of Jake so easily, and known the truth of Jake's empty, lonely life so clearly, effortlessly withstanding the lies Jake threw at him. The painful effect of being forced to see the truth of himself was overwhelming. In this painful truth was born within Jake a greater desire to run away, or to destroy the messenger of the truth that forced him to confront himself.

At that moment, Jake was remembering the scuffle at the store, and how John stepped between him and the line of fire toward Seth Templeman. He remembered falling down the cellar stairs, unable to stop his own momentum, and the twist of fear he had felt when he realized he was going to fall. He remembered clearly, too clearly, the horrible cracking pop his spine made as he had rolled head over heels to the bottom of the steps, crashing against the cement wall. And the shock at feeling nothing past that one horrific burning wrench as he crunched down at the bottom. The terror of not being able to feel, or to move, or to do anything at all.

Most of all, he remembered the gentle eyes of John, looking down at him with compassion and concern. No one had looked at him like that since he had been a little boy in his mother's arms. The memory caused his eyes to burn, and his heart and soul to warm. It frightened Jake. He quickly pushed the memory away from him, confused and embarrassed. It was a sign of weakness to feel this way, and he was strong. He didn't need anyone, ever!

Jake didn't know what John had done to him, but he figured that he must have been in some kind of shock from falling down the stairs, and then just naturally came out of it. No need to be grateful for that, he scoffed. Just nature, taking its course. That guy John was trying to play head games and make him believe he had fixed Jake's back. Probably trying to psych him out, or something.

Jake sat on the crate flicking a lighter to flame, shutting off the fuel, and then lighting it again. After a few moments, he picked up an old hamburger wrapper from the floor and idly lit it. He held it until the very last minute before it would have burned his fingers and then dropped it to the floor. In that seemingly trivial action an evil plan was spawned. The enemy of all that is good, the evil force in the universe, surely exulted that night.

Jake lit his lighter again and held his free hand over the flame until he could feel it burning his flesh. When the normal self-preservation voice inside of him cried out for him to move his hand away from the danger, he ignored it; in fact, he laughed. He was tough—he could handle it. His flesh reddened, seared, and began to blacken. "Let's see how tough you are, John!" he laughed.

Chapter Sixteen

Marriane Larson glanced at the clock on the bedside table near her and saw that it was almost 10:30 P.M. Although she had felt generally better since her release from the hospital after the accident, she was now pale and covered in sweat. Her husband, Jimmy, had gone out to help someone who lived quite a ways out of town, and was not due back for another hour or so. She was feeling worse by the minute and sorely wished he was with her. The pain in her side was making it difficult to breathe normally, and at times she felt like someone was ripping apart her insides in a searing grasp.

Marriane was not someone to complain. There had been times during this first pregnancy when her husband had almost begged her to take it easier. Right now, though, she would gladly have accepted some help. Since the accident, she had felt uneasy about the unborn baby inside of her. The doctor had said everything was fine, and yes, she had received a blessing, but in some strange way Marriane had felt different than she did before the accident. Something wasn't right, and was getting less right by the second.

Another jab of pain tore into her, and Marriane groaned deeply. The baby was not due for another five weeks. At first, she consoled herself that this could be a premature delivery, but when another hard pain hit her again she accepted the truth: something was very wrong with her, and with her child.

As Marriane doubled over with another pain, her water broke. Her fingers slowly made their way down to touch the fluid. When she brought her hand back up, she saw with horror that it was covered with blood.

The phone was beside her on the bedside stand, but it seemed to be miles away. When she was finally able to reach over and pick it up, she dialed Terrell and Shirley's number. Her head was swimming and the numbers were blurred. "Hello, Mom? My water broke, but there's a lot of blood with it," was all she managed to say before she fell back unconscious on the bed, dropping the phone to the floor.

Frantic, Shirley called into the phone, "Marriane? Marriane!"

But there was no answer.

Chapter Seventeen

While Nathan was riding along with cute and funny Suzie, he didn't mind that he was heading back to Crystal, and his parents. In the back of his mind, he figured there was plenty of time to hitch a ride elsewhere. When Suzie dropped John and him off at the boarding house where John lived, Nathan was quick to start heading out for parts unknown.

"Where are you heading?" asked John.

"Anywhere but here!" replied Nathan without looking back.

"You know, you could always spend the night and take off again in the morning," John suggested.

Nathan turned around on that one and with some irritation shot back, "I already got you figured, man! You want me to fix things up with my parents; they sent you to bring me back, didn't they? But I'm not going to. I don't plan on living their way anymore. I tried it, I didn't like it. It's my life now. That's it!"

"No, Nathan, your folks didn't send me. Like I said, how about if you just spend the night at my place, and then you can take off in the morning if you want to. I don't live in anything fancy, but it's warm—which is a lot more than you can say for what you usually stay in."

Nathan was chewing on that when a deputy sheriff drove up. Rolling down his window, the deputy leaned out and asked, "You're John, aren't you?"

"Yes, I am."

"Terrell Larson asked us to find you. Seems there's a family emergency at the hospital. I guess he wants you to come quick, so hop in and I'll give you a ride over there."

John started to get in and said to Nathan, "Come with me." Nathan started to resist, then noticed the deputy looking him over pretty close. Here we go again, thought Nathan. All things considered, it seemed wiser to go along until later when things cooled off, so he got in.

* * *

The first thing John saw as he entered the hospital waiting room with Nathan was Terrell's anguished face. At the sight of the two young men, Terrell left the circle of family and came over, taking both John's hands in his. Gripping them tightly, Terrell said, "Thank you for coming. Marriane's in trouble. I guess the baby started to come early, and there were complications. She's lost a lot of blood. Things don't look too good." Tears welled up in Terrell's eyes. "It shouldn't have happened this way, you know. It's because Skoggins ran them off the road."

"The baby is in trouble too, isn't it?" said John quietly, hoping to change the subject away from Jake.

"Yes," nodded Terrell. He started to say more, shook his head, turned back toward the couch where he dropped down heavily. Shirley put an arm around his shoulders and attempted to comfort her husband, even though her own eyes were filled with worry. In their hurt, Shirley, who was usually open and upfront, had pulled back into herself, while Terrell, normally easy-going, was nursing a bitter anger.

Nathan was miserable and out of place with all this emotional tension, with people he didn't even know. Besides, he hated hospitals—the smells, the noises, the frightening sense of everything being out of control. At least, out of his control. Looking around, he found a chair in an unused corner near a Coke machine and hid behind a magazine.

Jimmy said to John, "Marriane is in surgery. They're trying to stop the bleeding."

As he spoke to John, his face was drained with pain and fear. "The nurse said she lost a lot of blood before she got to the hospital." He tried to say more, tears pouring down his cheeks, but the words got stuck in his throat and refused to come out. "Excuse me," he finally choked out. He turned away and walked over to the window to be alone for a while.

John could feel this family's faith weakening. They were good people. They trusted in God, and they were struggling. They needed help, and they needed it now!

John excused himself and went out to talk with someone at the nurses' station. When he came back into the waiting room, he said, "We have permission to use an empty patient room. Terrell, do you want to call your family together to pray for Marriane?"

Terrell's eyes focused slowly. He seemed to come from far away, as if out of a cold, lonely fog, but he came, and nodded his assent. "Come on, everyone. Let's go have a prayer for Marriane," he said. The group started coming together, filing slowly out of the waiting room.

John looked around for Nathan and found him slumped back in a chair, flipping through a magazine, not really reading it. "Nathan," he said, "stick around until I'm finished here, okay? Here's five bucks, there's a cafeteria down the hall, and you can get some dinner."

Nathan shrugged, taking the money. What the heck, he might as well eat. But after that, if he could find a ride back to town, he'd go!

When the Larsons had gathered in the room, John closed the door. There was an awkward silence as John gave Terrell the opportunity to take his rightful place as the patriarch in the family, and lead the family in a humble petition to God in behalf of Marriane. But Terrell stood with his head down, not speaking. As if he felt John's insistent gaze, Terrell looked up at John and said, "I can't, I just can't! I've got the wrong spirit. I'm too angry—I just can't. If you don't mind, Jimmy, I'll ask John to give the prayer."

Jimmy nodded his head, and everyone knelt in a semi-circle as best the room and its furniture would allow. "Your prayer will be heard," Terrell said to John, "I'm sure it will." John looked into Terrell's eyes and tried to send the message, "Believe."

Taking a deep breath, John bowed his head and began to pray.

Chapter Eighteen

After everyone had gone back to the lounge to await further news, Dr. Macy came in. His operating scrubs were covered with small specks of blood. Marriane's blood, thought Jimmy, sick at heart. Jimmy, Shirley, and Terrell crowded around Dr. Macy to hear what he had to say, while John remained on the couch out of respect for the family. "There were complications that we couldn't compensate for," said the doctor. "The loss of blood from the separation of the placenta before she arrived at the hospital put extreme stress on the child. I'm sorry, but we couldn't save your daughter, Jimmy."

Shirley bit down hard on her lip and turned away. Jimmy's face was pale as he tried to comprehend the loss of his tiny unborn daughter. In contrast, Terrell's face was flushed with anger and frustration. He began to speak, but Jimmy came to himself and jumped in first. "Marriane? How is she, Doc? She's all right?"

The doctor dropped his eyes before answering, "Your wife is in critical condition. She is very weak and is not responding well to the blood transfusions we've given her. It will be a while before we know how well she'll react to the surgery. Are there other family members that need to be notified of her condition?"

"Her parents are both dead. Her sister lives in Canada," said Jimmy mechanically. "I called her, but she has a heart problem and can't come."

The doctor began to say something else about Marriane's medical condition, but he stopped, seeing the pain in the eyes of these people who loved his patient. "I'll make sure you are kept aware of any change in her condition. She is being made as comfortable as possible." The doctor put his hand on Jimmy's shoulder. "She's still in post-op," he said, "but as soon as we can, I'll get you in to see her."

Jimmy nodded his thanks, turned, and walked back over to the window that looked out on a nearly empty parking lot. He looked, but he did not see. His heart was beating, but he had stopped living.

The doctor started to leave, but Terrell quickly stepped beside him to speak. Together they talked in hushed tones for a few minutes, then Terrell returned to the others. His face was unreadable, but his eyes spoke volumes. His anger bordered on hate, and he was consumed with a spirit that should not have been there.

John rose from the couch and came to Terrell. "What did the doctor say?" asked John.

Pounding his right hand into his left, Terrell looked directly at John. "It's Skoggins' fault. It was because of the accident. The impact of the crash tore the place where the baby was growing inside of her, and it just got worse. It was that low-life Skoggins that killed our baby; and now maybe even Marriane. He does whatever he wants, and gets off with a slap on the hands. He's out walking the streets right now, free and easy, while the innocent . . ." A sob tore itself free of Terrell's throat before he caught himself with a start. "I'm going to make sure that justice is done this time!"

John reached out and put his hand around the back of his friend's shoulder to comfort him. "Bishop, the Lord knows what has gone on here. He has not forgotten this family, nor is He asleep. Let Him bring true justice to pass. And be at peace about your granddaughter; she is with her Savior now."

Terrell stood motionless as a tremendous battle took place within him. He could feel the strength and power of the Spirit of God in this man before him, who he was beginning to believe was an apostle of the Lord Jesus Christ. All his life, and especially since joining the Church, Terrell had lived by trusting in the promises of divine assistance and the power of hope. He had taught it to others, bearing testimony of his belief in it untold times. But the feelings of pain and injustice, and his own inadequacy to bring about justice with his own hands, called up the shreds of self-pride that had lain unnoticed and hidden in dark and dusty corners of his mind until now.

Through the mists of anger and pain came a vision of the words on a poster that hung in Terrell's home next to the bathroom mirror: "Just when I think that I have fully surrendered, then He asks me for something I don't want to give up." At this thought, huge tears welled up in Terrell's eyes as he bowed his head and sobbed. John reached out to enfold Terrell in his arms, and they stood together in silence.

Chapter Nineteen

The clock in the small country hospital's Intensive Care unit read 1:34 A.M. Marriane's physical condition had stabilized in recovery, but she had not regained consciousness. The coma she had slipped into had drawn a shadow over the lives of the Larson family and decreased most of the interest they had in the Christmas holiday, now only twelve days away.

Terrell, John, and Jimmy sat in the room where Marriane lay. Shirley had finally gone home to look after the younger children. The IV in Marriane's arm was hooked to a device that blinked with every drop. Her heart rate was monitored and displayed on a screen above the bed. She looked pale and faded, almost as if she was only partially in this dimension of reality, and partially somewhere else. A heavy quiet filled the room.

Teresa appeared in the doorway and took in the scene. The sight of her sister-in-law, usually so full of life and laughter, now so deathly still, caught at her breath. She went to Jimmy and put her hand on his arm. "I'm sorry, Jimmy. I wish there was something I could do." Jimmy smiled weakly and squeezed her hand before dropping his chin back into his hands and focusing back on his wife. Teresa looked around for a seat, but finding none, took a place against the wall where she too could watch over Marriane.

John saw that his time to leave had come, so he excused himself, promising to return in the morning. In the waiting room, he found Nathan asleep, curled up in a chair in the corner. John watched him for a moment, noticing how innocent the boy looked in his sleep. If only he could let himself stay that way, thought John.

John reached over and shook Nathan gently until he roused. "Wha—? What do you want?" he asked in a groggy voice.

"Let's go, guy. You can spend the night at my place." John gently helped the still half-asleep Nathan to his feet and out the door of the waiting room. They walked quietly down the hall and out the door into the night.

* * *

Nathan was invited to, and gladly took, the only bed in John's room at the boarding house. Within minutes, he was asleep. A sleeping bag became both a place to kneel in prayer and bed for John.

After his prayer, John looked for several minutes at Nathan. "Good night, Nathan, sleep well," he said with a grin. Then he snuggled down and gave into God's hands the events of this very long day.

Chapter Twenty

Henrietta Turnsen gasped for breath. The emphysema she had suffered from the past five years, and which her doctor had told her would likely end her life soon, was reaching up and choking her. She should have quit smoking a long time ago, but she was darned if she was going to let some "wet-behind-the-ears-kid-doctor" who was only forty-seven tell her how to run her life. Besides, she was getting old, so what could anyone expect? Let them see how full of pep they'd be when they had been around as long as she had!

Reaching over to turn on the light by her bed, she knocked down the book she had been reading before bedtime. As it hit and skidded across the hardwood floor, Henrietta started to sit up. But she was met with a feeling of lightheadedness, and then found that she could barely breathe. For a moment, fear crept into her mind, but she dismissed it with an audible, "Oh, fudge!" and then made another attempt to sit up.

With all the strength she had in her old, wiry body, Henrietta twisted herself into a sitting position on the side of her four poster cannon ball bed. She put out her left hand and held on to the headboard for support, resting for a moment. I just need to get up and sit in my rocker for a while, she thought. That's always helped before.

As she attempted to rise, her legs melted under her and she slid down the side of the bed to the floor. She tried to laugh at herself, grumbling, "Now, I . . . can't . . . even . . . get out . . . of bed!" But as flippant as she tried to sound, she knew she was in serious trouble. She lived alone, liked it that way, but that also meant no one would be coming around or wondering about her for a long time. Her help knew better than to come knocking on her door. It might be late tomorrow evening before anyone checked to see why she wasn't about. As much as it hurt her pride, she knew she needed to call for help.

Even sitting on the floor, she was feeling weaker by the moment. Things seemed foggy, hazy to her, as if someone had stuffed cotton in her head, so fuzzy and disconnected was she becoming. Reaching over to pick up the phone took forever, and it was hard to remember the number of the hospital.

"Hello . . . this is . . . Henrietta Turnsen. I'm having some problems . . . Have Dr. Jaffery call me!" While she listened to what the person on the other end of the line was saying, she concentrated hard on breathing. "What ? . . . Oh, he knows my number . . . just tell him. Thank you." This done, she clumsily placed the phone receiver back in the rest and closed her eyes.

So what now? she thought to herself. Then a thought came slowly and quietly into her heart: "Pray." She had not prayed formally to God for almost seventy-eight years now. Through all kinds of troubles and turmoil, strife, and heartache, Henrietta had kept her own counsel and believed in her own abilities. She had kept the truth of her own vulnerabilities and weaknesses under cover and out of her mind. She had spent a lifetime laughing at the thought that she needed God to help her.

Yet into this calloused old woman's life and heart had come a very special man. Through him, she had been able to face at least a part of her hurt and had come to know she could walk through her pain. She had also caught a glimmer of and allowed a touch of . . . what? the love of God?! A small crack in her walls had opened up to release some of the infection of self-loathing she had carried these many years. With every bit of hurt she had given up, she had received peace and calm within her soul. For such is the ecology of Heaven, that for every piece of hurt given freely and openly to God, an exchange is made and an equal amount of wholeness is given in its place. Henrietta was learning this, and she had increasingly been living it.

From this place of quiet, Henrietta now looked slowly toward God. Her eyes closed and her mind cleared as she hesitantly said, "God . . . John says you're there. He told me . . . you care about people like me, and that you like to help when someone is in trouble." For a moment she paused and then continued, "Now, I still don't understand why you let that happen to me when I was little, and part of me still is kind of mad about me trusting in you and still bein' hurt like that. But if you're willin', then I'm willin' to let you have another chance from this point on. So how about you help me out with all this . . . lung stuff . . . right now?"

Not a second later the phone rang beside her so loudly she jumped. Picking up the phone, she found that somehow, her breathing had eased a bit. To Dr. Jaffery, she ruefully admitted, "I'm . . . it's my breathing again." And to his scolding, she answered, "I know, I know, you've been telling me that forever! . . . yes, I am willing to take this seriously now."

A wave of deep fatigue and drowsiness washed over her as she almost dropped the phone; her grip on it was weakening fast. When she could think a little clearer, she held up the receiver to her ear again to find a very concerned doctor.

"What?" she asked. "I . . . I just felt tired for a moment, that's all. No, I don't want you to . . . can't you just . . . ? Oh all right, have it your way. But I still think it's all a big deal over nothing."

To the doctor's warning to stay put, she replied with a touch of sarcasm, "Of course I'll be right here when the ambulance comes. Where you do think I'll be, Sam, out plowing up my fields?" She set the phone back down and closed her eyes.

The floor was not getting any softer, so she tried to rise again but without any more success than the first time. The ache in her left hip got her thinking about pain, which leapfrogged in her mind somehow to praying. She remembered she had been praying for help when the phone had rung.

Closing her eyes again, more out of an old childish habit than any understanding of reverence, she began praying again. "Well, that was fast. 'Course anyone could explain it as just a coincidence; I had already called my doctor. But, my breathing's feeling considerable better so's I could at least talk to the man . . . " She paused a moment as the thought came to her. "And Sam has never called back that fast before!"

She mulled that one over and said, "Okay, I'll give you that one. So how about you get that ambulance here quick? This floor is getting harder by the minute. And my old bones ain't no feather pillow to sit on."

Then she opened her eyes and prepared to wait. Until they got here, she would just concentrate on breathing easy and figuring out what she was going to do with those chickens in the north lot that weren't laying like they should be.

Chapter Twenty One

Nathan tossed and turned in bed. He was sweating heavily and his breathing came in erratic gulps. His heart beat rapidly as he tensed and flexed his muscles in response to things only he could see.

Nathan was being chased, and he was running for his life! There were dark figures following after him that he could not shake no matter what trick or effort he tried. In the dream, which he did not know was a dream, he was looking over his shoulder at fire-filled eyes as the dark figures pursued him.

He ran past some people and stopped to ask for their help, some place where he could hide and be safe, but they acted as if he wasn't there. He ran on, and saw that the black figures pursuing him took no notice of those he had tried to talk to.

Next to the bed, John lay in his sleeping bag on the floor. After he had listened to the boy's turmoil and fear for a time, he unzipped the bag to rise and kneel in prayer for a moment before turning to the troubled boy in the bed. Very gently John placed his hands on Nathan's head, and a presence beyond this world filled the room.

Nathan, meanwhile, was losing ground to the evil that stalked him. He dashed around a corner only to find himself in a dead-end alley. There was no way out. There was no place to hide. His eyes searched in vain. He knew this was the end.

A cold, unearthly sound shrieked out behind him. Whirling

around, he found himself face to face with several black figures that slowly moved toward him. His body was chilled and his heart seemed to stop beating. If he was breathing at all he did not notice.

Very carefully, a circle was formed with him in the middle. Nathan himself was the prey that would soon be devoured. In a brief moment of clarity in the midst of his terror, Nathan realized, So this is how I end. All the big dreams and get-rich-plans end like this. The circle drew smaller about him, and Nathan's only thought was a fevered hope that the end would not hurt too much. With a hideous wail the dark figures rushed as one at him.

Nathan's cry for help was the voice of a little child, a voice from long ago when he still believed and trusted in a loving Father in Heaven. From deep within his heart, in a chamber long forgotten and overlooked, a voice came forth and pleaded, "Please help me, God!"

The expected pain never came. There was a sound of scuffling and blows, more grunts and someone fell on Nathan. He squirmed out from under the heavy burden to see . . . his father? His father was battling furiously with three of the dark figures while the other two lay sprawled out on the ground.

Shocked and surprised, Nathan called out, "Dad?"

One of the attackers turned and grabbed hold of Nathan. Nathan saw his father burst past two others and throw yet another against an alley wall where it fell heavily, not to rise again. From behind Nathan's father, the other attackers rushed him. There was a flash of steel, and Nathan saw his father fall to the ground.

"No!" Nathan cried. "That's enough. No one does that to my dad!" In those few moments Nathan's heart changed. All thoughts of his own pain and needs were gone; he cared only about his father now.

Grabbing a long, rusty pipe that lay in the alley trash, Nathan began to swing it wildly at the two remaining attackers, who suddenly vanished into the darkness.

Nathan stood, looking for the dark forms and finding none. A heavy weariness took him as he turned to his father. As Nathan walked towards him, he saw his mother cradling his father's head in her lap. She stroked Harry's cheek and looked up at Nathan in grief. Harry was dying, and he had given his life for Nathan, the son that had rejected them, thrown their love away, and yet had been saved by that love.

As his father's eyes closed for the last time, his mother bowed her head and wept. Nathan stood in agony, powerless once again. Guilt and shame swept over him and he choked on the tears that overflowed his eyes. He was consumed by the grief from suddenly understanding what he had once had. And what he had now lost.

Great sobs rose and broke within him over and over again like waves on an empty beach. He forgot who or what or where he was in his misery, until spent and worn, he fell to his knees and buried his head in his arms.

* * *

Nathan slowly awoke and opened his eyes to find that he was being held by John. In the light of the moon, Nathan could see the moisture of his tears glistening on this kind and caring man's arm. Embarrassed, he looked into John's eyes, but saw only compassion and understanding. John smiled. "I know about your dream. We can talk in the morning about it. For now, get some sleep." Not completely understanding, but feeling comforted and safe, Nathan sighed and nodded before lying back down and falling fast asleep.

Chapter Twenty Two

It hadn't really snowed yet that year, and Christmas was only a few days away. People do more shopping for the holiday when it looks like Christmas, thought Seth. It was early yet, as he peered down the street and noted which homes along the way still were dark and which showed signs of life. Seth prided himself on his knowledge of the people in his town, saw it as part of being a good merchant. You have to know them better than they know themselves, he always said, or how are you going to sell them anything?

Seth usually saw the lights come on and people stirring because he rose early and worked from first light to the end of day. Ever since his wife Joyce had died, he had put one foot in front of another, day after day, week after week, month after month, and year after year. It was better that way. It kept him from really looking at the loneliness inside of himself.

The past few months though, this quick shuffle away from his feelings had not been working. At odd moments, like this one, an image, a sense of missing her, remembrances of what she smelled like when she was all dressed up to go out, what it felt like to hold her, kept peeking out. It was like putting away in the attic photos of someone you missed too much to look at every day, and then finding them sitting on the kitchen table one night. It was like making peace, sort of, with losing the big race, and then finding yourself back running it again, over and over.

She had been good to him. She wasn't a saint; she would admit to a temper at times. Joyce would also have told you that she didn't let most people get too close to her. But she loved Seth Templeman with a strong and forgiving love that he missed down deep in his soul.

He was right in the middle of remembering the feel of her hand on his cheek when he noticed the police car go around the corner by Jackson's gas station. That will be Ed, thought Seth as he pulled out of his memories. Looking down at his watch and then back toward the disappearing patrol car, he mused, "A little late this morning. He must have fallen asleep again sitting out along the highway."

It was almost 7 A.M. now, and most of the homes along the street had at least one light on. Seth always nodded his head approvingly at this wake-up call that he symbolically had issued, before turning back to putter around the store until he was "officially" open for the day. It was Wednesday, so he got out his feather duster and began his routine. After doing this for so long the same way, he hardly even saw what was actually before him. So he hardly noticed that one cabinet was slightly ajar.

Automatically he started to push it shut and go on to other things when something touched his awareness, and he stopped. I always make sure all the cabinets are shut before I close up and leave, thought Seth. He pursed his lips thoughtfully as he mentally considered the contents of this cabinet in particular before opening it up to look inside. This was where he stored the flares—big ones, small ones, the kinds you use to signal an accident on the highway, or maybe just use to make a long sustained light on the fourth of July. Seth didn't sell many.

Checking carefully, he found that five of the big ones were gone. The places where they had sat were evident by the lack of dust in those five narrow slots in the rack. Seth checked under the rack in the cabinet, opened up some boxes that were stacked below, and then stared at the place where the five flares should be. Next he went over to the counter, and laying down the feather duster next to the cash register, reached up to the shelf where the ledgers were kept and opened up a big green book. Turning to a particular page and scanning the numbers for a while, he finally said out loud to himself, "I knew it! I haven't sold any of those since last June."

Slamming the ledger book shut with an emphatic bang, he tossed it onto the counter and started back to the cabinet where the missing flares should have been. On the way, another thought came to him, so he bypassed the cabinet and went down the cellar stairs to check it out.

The front part of the cellar was kept pretty clean and tidy, as it held only the goods that Seth sold a lot of. The back part, on the other hand, was just for personal things he and Joyce had collected over the years. A lot of it was filled with her clothes, the thousands of books that she enjoyed so much but which Seth never found time to read himself and hadn't the heart to give away, and his own fishing gear from days long gone.

Seth never went to the back part of the cellar, so he had never paid any attention to its small door in the far wall. That door had been chained shut since before he bought the place twenty-five years ago. It took some doing to even find the light back there, and then to climb over, around, and move out of the way all the stuff that blocked his path. The closer he got to the back wall, the colder the air became.

When he moved the last box, Seth stopped dead in his tracks. The door had been smashed in half! Obviously, whoever had forced it open had not cared much about anyone finding out about it. Examining the doorjamb, Seth saw the recently made gashes in the wood. Someone had tried to pry off the hasp and failing that, had just decided to kick in the door.

When Seth got back upstairs, he called the sheriff's office and reported the break-in.

"Anything missing?" asked the deputy who took the report.

"Well, all I've noticed so far was some big, heavy-duty flares," Seth answered.

The deputy was surprised. "What would anybody do with flares?"

"Oh, a lot of things, I suppose," Seth mused. "For instance, you sure could start one heck of a fire with them, that's for sure!"

Chapter Twenty Three

Nathan woke slow and easy. He lay in bed for almost ten minutes, looking at the ceiling and enjoying the sensation of peace and relaxation he was feeling. His heart was more whole and at peace than it had been for a long time. He was not afraid anymore.

John sat quietly in the wicker chair by the window, watching Nathan. He knew that this young boy had been full of fears for so long that he had forgotten what it was like to just "be." People who are fearful all the time, thought John, have a nagging, uneasy feeling that covers them like a heavy, suffocating blanket. They don't get to sit in the cool of the evening and let the breeze flow over them. They can't laugh until their sides hurt with someone who likes them. They aren't able to let morning come gently to them, and welcome it joyously. Most of all, they can't let in the love God offers to them, especially when it comes to them through the imperfections of other mortal beings.

Nathan gave a full-body stretch that reached every muscle and sinew from the top of his head all the way down to the ends of his toes. When he saw John sitting by the window, he blinked in surprise. "Uh, hi," was all he could manage to say.

"Morning!" said John in return. "How about some breakfast? I know the best place in town to eat. Umm gooood, I smell the pancakes and eggs already!"

"Yeah, okay. That sounds good. Just give me a minute to get my pants on and use the bathroom," said Nathan with a shy smile. He was feeling very differently toward John now than when he first met him, but he still felt a little awkward about showing it so openly. If John didn't bring up anything about his crying last night, it was okay with him.

While Nathan was in the shared bathroom down on the next level of the old house, John waited for him. "You know," John spoke casually through the door, "I had quite a dream last night. I was walking along this . . . do you believe in dreams, Nathan?"

Nathan answered thoughtfully, "Yeah . . . I think I do."

John smiled to himself and continued. "Anyway, there I was in this dream. I was walking along and this guy was being chased into an alley by these dark figures. So in my dream I decided to see if I could help and took off running after them." John stopped at this point, listened for a moment, and knocked on the door. "You still there, Nathan?"

Inside the bathroom, Nathan was throwing water on his face and wondering how John knew about his dream. He shook his head and replied, "I'm still here."

"So there I am in this alley, and I run up on all these people, and . . . what do you suppose is going on?"

"A fight?" came the voice out of the bathroom.

"Hey, good guess! So anyway, I think maybe I need to jump in and help this poor guy on the ground. But then I see someone else, an older man, jump in there and start taking care of the bad guys. He was really impressive for his age."

Nathan came out of the bathroom and gave John a strange look as the two of them went down the stairway, down the hallway and out of the door. All the while John didn't miss a beat as he talked.

John continued to describe "his dream," and when he told Nathan how the older man had died to save his son, Nathan felt his heart sink all over again. "I felt really bad for the older guy," said John. Nathan kept walking along with his eyes downcast and shoulders drooping.

John stopped talking and the two walked along in that silence so full of feeling that words only get in the way. When it felt right to him, John reached over and put his arm around Nathan's shoulders. "I could tell in my dream that the younger guy really cared about this older fellow. They could almost have been father and son."

Nathan fought back the tears, but there was just too much emotion. His eyes grew teary and his heart felt warm and full. When he looked up, he saw that John knew, understood, and loved without any judging. They walked along together in silence for almost a mile.

* * *

The little brown wooden house with the porch swing appeared and got larger as the two of them came around the corner and walked toward it. Nathan was so preoccupied with his own thoughts that he didn't recognize his own family's home until he was actually going up the steps. Then his old self jumped out, seeing a danger to his free and easy ways.

"Wha . . . wait! What are we doing here? I thought you said we were going to go somewhere and eat?"

John nodded, shrugged his shoulders and replied, "This place has the best food in town. I figured, nothing but the best for my friends!"

Nathan started to turn and flee when the front door opened and his mother came out. "Nathan?" she said softly, her voice filled with both gladness and caution. She wanted to believe this miracle could actually be happening, but she had been hurt too much already to fully give herself to it yet.

"Hi . . . Mom." Nathan looked sideways at John, whose eyes were smiling.

"It's okay, Nathan," John encouraged as if answering an unspoken question.

Janet came toward Nathan and hesitantly touched him on the arm. "Would you like to come in?" she asked softly and hopefully.

Nathan experienced a lifetime's worth of thinking, feeling, weighing, and evaluating in that moment. His eye was caught by some movement in the window behind his mother, and he was surprised to see an orange and white kitten staring out at him. His inner battle over for the moment, he felt free enough to be the peaceful, happy Nathan that God had always intended for him to be.

"Yeah, Mom, I thought I would see what was for breakfast." When he smiled at Janet, her heart threw off its protective cover and she reached out to rejoice in her only son's return. Her arms wrapped him in as much of a hug as her swollen, pregnant belly would allow, and her eyes were awash in tears. All those prayers, all those dreams, all the hoping that somehow, some way, God would find him and reunite the family had come full circle.

As Janet and Nathan turned to go arm in arm into the house, she looked at John over Nathan's head. "Thank you," she whispered.

John said, "God does good work, huh?" He smiled. "I have to get going now, but I'll check in on you all tonight, okay?" He made to leave, but Janet ran after him before he could get very far and gave him a hug and kiss. It was a happy man that left them. John was filled with the special kind of joy that is a side benefit of being an instrument in the hands of the Lord.

Chapter Twenty Four

Terrell Larson sat beside the bed of his comatose daughter-in-law. The hospital sounds and smells surrounded him but he was oblivious to all, alone inside himself where his anger raged. He had encouraged Jimmy, who was exhausted by the strain of the past thirty-six hours, to get some sleep. "You might as well get some shut-eye," Terrell had said. "I won't be able to sleep anyway." So while Jimmy slept uneasily in a chair in the corner, Terrell sat next to the hospital bed, lost in his thoughts, lost in his anger.

It's not supposed to happen this way, he thought to himself, and to God. You work hard, you trust in God, and things are supposed to work out. Maybe when you need the opportunity to practice living the commandments better, then things are allowed to get a little crazy, but not this. This girl hasn't done anything to deserve this.

Terrell stood and walked over to the window, looking out but not really seeing. The sun was up now, but the day seemed dim and overcast to him. Terrell rubbed his unshaven face with his hands and ran them through his silver-streaked hair.

A voice behind him said, "He never said it would be easy."

Terrell turned to see who had spoken, but he already half knew before he saw John standing beside the bed. The two of them looked at each other for a moment until Terrell came to the other side of the bed and looked down at Marriane. "I must seem pretty shallow in my faith right now," he said. "All the counsel I've given to people about trusting in the wisdom and love of God, and still I struggle with my own testimony. Some bishop I am!"

"Oh, I don't know about that," John said. "You're still very much a mortal, human being, who hasn't yet come to fully know that God's perfect plans always come to pass. I think you're being a mite hard on yourself. After all, God already knows your heart and what you truly believe in. It's you that still doesn't know for sure. You and Abraham, that's what it looks like to me. Probably have the same kind of final outcome as well."

Terrell reached over and brushed a bit of Marriane's hair away from her closed eyes. Looking up at John, he asked, "Do you ever struggle to believe, to trust?"

Now it was John who went to look out the window. He knew what his answer was, but he wanted to find the right words to express the vast and rich feelings this question touched in him. Memories of the many, many years of living and striving to be true to the truths his Lord and best friend had taught him as they tramped the dusty hills of Galilee flooded through him. Does someone who heard the truths of eternity spoken from the lips of the Son of God, and who has even been present when God himself has spoken, ever struggle to be completely spirit-centered?

John spoke slowly now, with a great deal of feeling and awareness of what his words must mean to this man. "Terrell, I know who you believe me to be. Trust me when I say that no matter who I am, or how far along the same road toward perfection I may be, or how far you may be, we all must travel the same difficult way. The struggle is still the same. Jesus himself never claimed to be perfect as is Heavenly Father until after He was resurrected. And I am far from being as perfect as Jesus was."

Terrell sat down in the chair by the bedside and looked at John, and then back down at Marriane. "But when you know, like you do, what will come to pass, doesn't it make it easier? Aren't you able to brush off any doubts or fears that come from not knowing?"

John turned from the window. "I'm not God. I don't know everything that will come to pass in people's lives." He chuckled softly and continued, "I don't even know all of what is going to happen in my own life. The broad outlines, sure, but all the details and setbacks that require my own growth to work through? No. My faith is only the focusing of my spirit to receive and expand with God's spirit. First I have to have some knowledge, then I link faith with it, which results in further knowledge coming to me. If it were a tangible item, it would look kind of like a chain, with alternating links of knowledge and faith, trials, blessings, trials, and so on. In some things my knowledge is perfect; it's not a question of faith. In others, I still don't know all there is to know. No mortal man can."

Terrell sighed deeply and slumped heavily in his chair. When he looked up again he said, "Is it hard for you to keep from doing . . . something that is wrong? Something no one else could see, even if it is only inside of you?"

John came around the bed and sat down in another chair next to Terrell. He shook his head slowly. "Doing wrong is not a problem anymore for me, inside or out. What is still imperfect in me is not doing all the good that I could. We sometimes call that 'sins of omission' rather than 'sins of commission.'" With a distant look in his eyes he said, "But I clearly remember wrestling with my own personal ideas about how life should be and what kind of justice God ought to enforce. What a poor God I would have made! Too much justice and not enough mercy, lots of toughness but too little tenderness, acceptance, and understanding." He turned to Terrell. "Do you see how all this is one big school for godhood?"

Terrell smiled weakly and nodded. "I sure hate some of the required courses!" he said.

"I understand," laughed John as he took his friend's hand and pulled them both up and out of the chairs. "Let's give Marriane a blessing. You anoint, and I'll seal and be mouth for the blessing." He reached over and gently woke Jimmy, who stood up quickly, his eyes blurry with exhaustion. As John guided the still waking young man to stand next to his wife and participate in the blessing, he continued, "Then I have a favor to ask of you."

Chapter Twenty Five

Terrell walked slowly down the hallway of the hospital toward Henrietta Turnsen's room. He hadn't even known she was there until John had told him. When he found out, and John asked him to be with her during the last few hours of her mortal life, Terrell had protested. It hadn't seemed right to leave Marriane. Then he had felt the old familiar feeling in his heart when the Spirit was talking to him. He had known that this was what the Lord wanted him to be doing right now, not sitting and brooding.

Terrell came to Henrietta's room and stood outside the door, thinking about what John had said to him. He had said, "Terrell, my friend, what we would do in our desires to do good is not always what is best. Just because we can help doesn't always mean we should. And those we think we are best suited to help are often better helped by someone else. Put aside your ideas about how it all should work, and trust God's plan."

Now Terrell stood outside Henrietta's door, trying to figure out just exactly what he was here to do and say. He could feel the soft but persistent touch of the Master's hand on his shoulder asking him to go and offer love. "I will give you what you need, as you need it" came the impression into his heart and mind. With that, Terrell entered the silent hospital room and left his own personal burdens behind at the door.

He half closed the door behind him and turned to see Henrietta lying in bed with an IV in her arm, a heart monitor, and an oxygen cannula in her nose to help her breathe. Physically she looked worn and frail; her old body was using up the last of its energies. Beyond that, there was a peacefulness about her that filled the darkened room and touched the still-lingering turmoil in Terrell. Her eyes were closed when he came into the room, but slowly opened, noticing him as he stood by the bed.

"Hello, Bishop. Are you all right?"

He had come to care for her and was taken off balance by the turn. "I . . . sure, I'm fine. How are you?" he stammered.

She smiled, closed her eyes and said, "John said you wouldn't want to talk about your own pain." She tried to breathe long and deep but instead began to cough. It took a few minutes to catch her breath, and then she opened her eyes and took him in. "He also told me I had something to offer you; something that only I could give. So go get yourself a chair and park it while we talk."

As Terrell brought a chair over, Henrietta began to cough again, hoarse, liquid-filled coughs that seemed to twist her lungs to shreds. Terrell didn't know what else to do, so he took her hand and sat there beside the bed until the coughing subsided.

When she could talk again, she jumped right into it. "I don't have a lot of time left. And don't try and feed me all that honey-covered baloney that the nurses here keep trying to give me about my getting better. My time is almost over, and I know it. But I'm ready for it. More ready than I ever thought I would be."

Terrell felt a lump growing in his throat and had the impression that what he was going to hear was very important. Henrietta paused to swallow back another fit of coughing before she continued.

"I spent most of my life," she said very deliberately, "being mad that life wasn't the way I thought it should be. I was mad at being hurt by other people and had made up my mind I wasn't going to let any-one hurt me again. I figured if I made myself tough enough, no one could get to me." Her eyes at that moment looked a bit like the old fiery, feisty woman that Terrell had known, but then they softened and looked deeply into his. "But I was wrong. It was all a lie. All of it! It don't work that way, and I guess deep down inside of me I knew that all along, but didn't want to admit it."

Tears came to her eyes and she squeezed his hand in hers with what strength she had left. "I wasted so much life pretending to be too tough to hurt, when what I really needed to do was to learn to heal better. That's what being strong really means in this life: admitting that you need people. It took me until almost the end of my life to see that being tough and hard doesn't block out pain, it only blocks out love."

She chuckled weakly. "I thought I was so smart, and all of you so foolish. When all along it was the other way around."

Terrell loosened his grip on her hand just a bit. He struggled against the truth being shown to him by the Spirit—the truth that he needed to let go of his anger toward Jake Skoggins.

"Terrell," said Henrietta softly, "The Lord has healed my heart from all the hurt I did to myself. What was done to me was nothing like the hurt from my own anger, the hurt I did to myself all these years. The God you told me about, the one you believe in so much, has taken it all away."

Terrell felt like a little child again. He was being flooded with memories of the grandmother he had loved so much. He remembered how she had taken him on her knee and hugged him when he had been pushed around and hurt by the bigger boys. She had held him close and rocked gently back and forth with him until his sobbing had stopped. She had talked about how God could patch up his knee and put happiness in his heart. That God takes away the hurts and puts in your heart, instead, a rainbow. Even now, after all these years, he smiled when he thought of the rainbow. How he had loved and missed her! No one else had been able to help him open his heart to let go of his hurts as she had.

When he came back from his memories and focused on Henrietta again, she almost seemed to look like his grandmother. There was a glow around Henrietta that Terrell could see and feel. And from that, he began to understand why the Lord, through John, had brought the two of them together. How the healing that both of them needed could be worked through each other.

"Would you pray with me, my friend?" asked Henrietta. "I'll just stay here, and let you do the kneeling and the praying part."

Terrell pushed back his chair, and still holding her hand knelt beside the bed. "Dear Lord, . . . we thank Thee for . . ." He paused and felt for what was right to say and finally said, "Thy love. For Thy love that heals us and lifts us up from the pains of this life. May we more fully take Thy hand in ours and trust that Thou knowest the way better than we do."

It was not a long prayer, but it said what was needed. When he finished, Terrell stood and looked down at Henrietta. Her eyes were closed, and her breathing gradually grew more faint until it stopped. A moment later the heart monitor over her bed began to show a flat line and gave out a muted buzz.

Terrell let go of her hand and placed it carefully by her side. He leaned over and gently kissed her forehead before turning and going quietly out of the room. A moment later a nurse came into the room, followed shortly thereafter by the doctor. They would determine she had died as she had wanted, quickly and quietly, without any heroic measures, then they would turn off the equipment and unhook the IV.

Chapter Twenty Six

He was tired, though his heart was strong in the Spirit. His mind was clear and focused on the eternal truths he had learned during his premortal life and throughout his long mortal probation. But his body was worn and weary with the effort of the past days, weeks, and months.

A huge yawn came over him. He raised his arms overhead and stretched, attempting to shake off the fatigue. *So maybe my head isn't as clear and focused as I want it to be,* he thought as he walked along the road away from the hospital. *Sometimes it all gets heavy. It's not that I doubt the worth of what I'm doing here. I know the Lord has given me to do what He truly knows is best for me and those I help.*

It could just be that I get too eager to help things along and run ahead of what the Lord would do. He always did tell me I was too anxious to get things going. John shook his head a little and smiled. *You would think that after almost 2000 years I would have learned better.*

As he walked, he kicked a stone along the road and watched it skip ahead. A memory of the Master seated beside the Sea of Galilee, surrounded by the twelve, came to him. "You would have wanted the creation of the world to only take three days instead of six, if we had let you," Jesus had said to John. "You would have said, 'Let's just leave out a few parts, and fill them in later if we have to!'" The Master had laughed and embraced John. "Someday you will understand why everything has its own pace. Why some things cannot be rushed."

Guess I still need practice on timing, John shook his head. That and feeding myself better. His stomach growled and he said out loud, "I'm starved. Time to eat!"

* * *

The next few days went by quickly for some, and not so quickly for others. The Morse family enjoyed a togetherness they had not known for a long time. Nathan allowed himself to be cared about by his parents, Janet and Harry. He opened up, let go of past differences of opinion, and found himself, to his surprise, enjoying the safe and secure home life his wandering street existence had not provided.

The Larson family, on the other hand, struggled to find the holiday spirit while they kept a somber vigil beside the hospital bedside of their dear one. Marriane's condition did not change. Shirley tried to begin holiday preparations, but had no heart for it; the decorations and traditional snacks were mostly absent from their home. Jimmy sat hour after hour, day after day beside his Marriane. Sometimes he talked to her, other times he read to her out of the scriptures. For long periods he just held her hand and prayed.

Terrell had come to a place in his life that he had seen others face, but had never experienced personally. He thought about something he had heard once on the local Christian radio station that he liked to listen to when he drove alone. A preacher had said that every follower of Jesus Christ at some time in his life comes to a place and time when he feels abandoned by God. What life presents to him, and what he feels called to do with it, just does not make sense. God seems far away. Most people do not come through this moment, the preacher had gone on to say, to use this experience to rise higher in faith and hope in God. Rather, they develop scar tissue and forever remain on the same level of belief. They are unable or unwilling to walk through the fire.

In the midst of this crisis of spirit, Terrell continued to struggle, despite John's reassurance and Henrietta's dying testimony. Terrell faced the greatest challenge to his trust and faith in God he had ever known. At this point, he still lingered next to the edge. Pride and anger remained in his heart.

* * *

Henrietta Turnsen had left a request in her will that Terrell Larson act as executor of her estate and affairs. She also wanted him to conduct a graveside service for her. Not having any relatives to notify, according to her written instructions, he thought it best to go ahead and have her funeral right away. So on Saturday, two days after her death and two days before Christmas, he stood before her casket waiting for those that had gathered to find a place around the grave.

A cold breeze moved through the naked branches of the old trees that stood as silent sentinels in the cemetery. Grass that was tired from the long summer, which would usually be covered with snow by now and allowed to sleep, lay as a worn, brittle carpet underfoot. A few groundskeepers could be faintly heard at the far end of the cemetery doing their winter preparation work. The slightest smell of wood smoke from down the hill in town made its way up to where the quiet group had gathered.

Standing in the sober, dark blue suit he always wore when he presided at funerals, Terrell repeatedly squeezed and relaxed his grip on the Bible in his hands. He looked at the felt-covered pine casket that held the mortal remains of Henrietta Turnsen. He saw the grave that had been hacked out of the cold, hard ground, and noticed the plain headstone with its brief notation.

Henrietta had made the arrangements for her funeral many months before, specifically requesting the "cheapest durn box" they had, since "it don't make any sense to buy something expensive when you're just going to bury it!" Terrell thought now how much like Henrietta the casket was. Simple, yet functional and effective.

You are born, you die. For some span of days in between, you live out your life and try to find happiness. Providing someone doesn't make things hard for you, he thought.

Terrell shook his head a little as he realized that his thoughts were heading for despair. He tried focusing on the moment, paying particular attention to the feel of the cold breeze on his face.

Terrell was interrupted from his personal thoughts and feelings when John tapped him on the shoulder and said, "I think we're all here now, Bishop. We can start whenever you're ready."

Terrell nodded and looked around at the faces of those who had come to pay their last respects to Henrietta. Standing beside John was

Shirley. He was glad she had come with him, though he knew it had been hard for her to let go of worrying about Marriane long enough to come.

A couple of the men who had worked for Henrietta were also there, but that was all. So few! thought Terrell. Do these few people represent the total souls she touched? What is the real measure of a person's life? he wondered.

Terrell had done eight funerals since he had been made bishop, but he had never gotten comfortable doing it. He always felt so inadequate trying to sum up someone's life.

Taking a deep breath, he began. "I thank you for coming to pay your respects to the memory of Henrietta Turnsen."

The wind whipped around them and blew some of his hair into his eyes. Brushing it back into place with his hand, Terrell continued. "The instructions she left were that this service be kept short and to the point. She said specifically that she didn't want anyone saying a lot of 'syrupy nonsense' about her just because she was dead now."

Terrell smiled and very softly said, "But I'm afraid this is one time she is not going to get her way. I have a few things to say, and I ask for your patience with me as I find the words to express my feelings."

Terrell opened his Bible, turned to a place he knew well, and began to read quietly. "Psalms 37:3-7. 'Trust in the Lord, and do good; so shalt thou dwell in the land, and verily thou shalt be fed. Delight thyself also in the Lord; and he shall give thee the desires of thine heart. Commit thy way unto the Lord; trust also in him; and he shall bring it to pass. And he shall bring forth thy righteousness as the light, and thy judgment as the noonday. Rest in the Lord, and wait patiently for him.'"

Terrell looked for a moment at the page, then closed the book to look at the casket. "Henrietta Turnsen spent most of her life filled with pain. In her childhood she was hurt badly by someone whom she trusted, and with whom she should have been safe. For the rest of her life she suffered from this unhealed hurt and pain. She covered over that pain with anger. She had the mistaken belief that it is possible to get so tough that no one could ever hurt you again. She fell into the trap so many of us step into by believing that defending, not healing, is the answer to this painful life. She was wrong." Terrell swallowed awkwardly as he remembered her final moments of life with him at the hospital. "She learned this not long before she died."

Terrell looked up and into the eyes of John. John's eyes were filled with a bright light; his face was calm, almost unreadable. Terrell felt a spirit of tremendous love and joy about him, that he wanted to give himself to—but he couldn't.

Looking back at the casket, Terrell continued. "Shortly before she died, Henrietta was given a very special blessing from God. The same God she blamed for her troubles these many years. But it was this same God who was standing right there with open arms when she finally turned back to Him and opened up her heart."

Terrell stopped now. His heart was trying to say something but his head kept interfering. Finally, after what seemed to him like a long silence, he began to speak again.

"I have come to know myself about feeling angry at the selfish and senseless hurt someone can inflict upon you. I have struggled to not take matters into my own hands and bring about what I saw as justice."

Opening up his Bible again to Psalms 37, he read out loud: "'Fret not thyself because of him who prospereth in his way, because of the man who bringeth wicked devices to pass. Cease from anger, and forsake wrath: fret not thyself in anywise to do evil.'"

As Terrell read, the air about the small group became very still. The cold breeze that had teased and run over and between them stopped. Terrell had closed the book and begun to speak when he looked up. His face paled and he stopped in mid-thought, his mouth hanging open. After a few awkward moments all eyes were focused on him as he stared. Shirley moved closer to him and took his arm, thinking he was overcome with emotion from all of the stressful events of the past few days. She could feel him trembling. Everyone waited for Terrell to master his emotions, as he continued to stare straight ahead, as if he were listening to something he couldn't quite accept. The minutes ticked by. Most of those about him waited, perplexed and uneasy.

As Terrell's silence went on, John stepped quietly to the coffin and took a flower from the wreath that had been laid upon it. Putting the flower up to his nose, he inhaled deeply its sweet fragrance. Only partly to distract attention from Terrell, he said, "I'd like to say a few things that are in my heart, if you'll allow me. Sometimes I think life is like this flower. It grew, it will die. In between these two occurrences, it was meant by God to give beauty and a sweet fragrance to the world around it. And while it will soon be only a memory of what it was . . . what a memory we will share. It will have touched the hearts of any of us who would let it.

"That is the lesson of life for us all: to be our own personal expression of God's love and goodness. And then, when we leave this life, sweet memories will keep giving love to those who remain." John looked around at each of those gathered there. For that one moment in time, their hearts were one.

John turned to Terrell and asked, "Shall I give a prayer to close, Bishop?" Still speechless for some reason unfathomable to the crowd, Terrell nodded gratefully, and John's eyes sent a loving message to his friend before he bowed his head.

"Our Father in Heaven, humbly we pray to Thee this day on behalf of Henrietta Turnsen, and those gathered here to honor her memory. We pray that she may find rest in Thee, and those of us who knew and cared about her will someday be reunited with her in Thy presence. Please comfort those who remain behind, and bless them that they might more fully unite with Thy spirit and find strength."

Chapter Twenty Seven

Christmas music playing in the living room mingled with aromas from the kitchen. Holiday desserts and treats had been made in great abundance. A large, brightly lit tree stood in the family room, and mounds of presents surrounded it like the snow that should have been by now, but wasn't, covering the ground outside. Stockings were hung on the fireplace mantel, mistletoe was strategically placed over the entrance by the front door, garland was wrapped up along the banister leading upstairs, and pine boughs had been placed on the open beams in the kitchen. Teresa sat beneath the tree, arranging the creche.

The phone rang once, then again before Teresa realized that no one was either around or willing to take it. "Got it!" she called to no one in particular as she hurried into the kitchen to answer the phone.

"Hello? . . . Uh . . . I'm not sure, I'll check." Putting her hand over the receiver, Teresa yelled, "Brennnnt!" After listening for a moment she put the phone back to her ear and resumed the conversation. "I thought he was here, at least he was a little while ago. Sure, I'll give him the message. Merry Christmas to you, too."

After she hung up, Teresa took a moment to write down a note for her fifteen-year-old brother and stuck it on his personal hook under the family bulletin board. Her duty in that matter done, she whirled around and took stock of what needed her attention now.

Her mother never liked to rush the Christmas season, so she

always refused to start putting up things right after Thanksgiving, the way some people do. As the years had gone by, the starting date for decoration had gotten closer and closer to Christmas day, until now it was down to only a week before, when it all went into high gear. On this, the day before Christmas Eve, Teresa rolled up her sleeves, dived into the boxes of Christmas things hauled down from the attic, and set to work on the still huge amount of undone holiday preparations.

The sound of a car door shutting outside caught her attention. Going over to the kitchen window, she looked out and saw that her parents were back from the funeral of Henrietta Turnsen. She also saw that John was with them. Familiar feelings of confusion flooded her heart as she went to open the front door for her parents. She saw immediately that her father was pale and vacant-eyed, his step hesitant and unsure.

"Dad, what's the matter?" Teresa asked.

John answered for Terrell. "Your father is just worn out, Teresa."

But Teresa ignored John and asked again, more insistently. "Dad, what's wrong?" When he said nothing, Teresa turned to her mother and pleaded to know, "What's happened?"

Shirley shook her head at Teresa and then continued to lead her pale and weary husband up the stairs. "There's just been a lot going on lately, and he's tired. I'm going to put him to bed now, and let him get some rest." With that, Shirley disappeared up the stairs and around the corner.

Teresa stood for a moment looking up, debating whether to follow them and press for more details or simply return to her Christmas preparations for the moment. So deep was she in thought that John's comment startled her.

"Teresa, you've done a great job on the house. Do you need some help?"

She suddenly noticed John standing next to her. "What? Oh, I. . . ," she stammered, shook her head "no," and abruptly ran into the kitchen where she took a deep breath before hurtling herself into a flurry of holiday baking.

As she gathered the necessary ingredients, she heard the door open and looked up to see her brother Brent.

"Mom and Dad home?" he asked. "Where are they?"

"Upstairs," she said shortly. "Resting."

"Why?" he asked with natural curiosity. "What's wrong?"

His simple question reminded her of how her mother had shut her out when she had tried to ask the same thing. "How do you expect me to know?" she said sharply. "Can't you see I'm busy?"

"Well, thanks for nothing!" he said as he left her to his work. She heard his voice as he apparently encountered John in the next room.

"Women! They're all nuts! All I did was ask if Dad was home, and she told me he was laying down because he wasn't feeling well. So I ask her what's the matter with him . . . and she yells at me! Women are all wackos!"

Teresa heard John's laugh as he replied. "How about you and I go finish cleaning out that part of the barn your Dad asked you to do last week. I imagine you could use some help with it." And then she heard the front door open and shut, leaving only silence behind.

She worked steadily, mixing and kneading, and was horrified to see tears falling into the dough. At the sound of footsteps on the stairs, she quickly brushed them away.

As her mother came into the kitchen, Teresa avoided looking directly at her although she watched closely as Shirley got a drinking glass out of the cupboard and filled it with water. Standing in front of the sink, she slowly took a long drink and stared out the window. The quiet settled around them like a heavy blanket. It wasn't a quiet of peace, but of turmoil.

"Mom, please tell me what's the matter with Dad," Teresa urged.

Shirley didn't answer.

"Mother, why don't you answer me?"

"Teresa, please!" said Shirley. Teresa heard the tiredness in her voice but also an exasperation that cut her to the heart. "Please just let it go for now. Even your father gets tired sometimes."

Teresa stopped kneading and looked hard at her mother, who was still in front of the sink, holding the glass and staring out the window. One voice inside of Teresa said to let it go, but another one begged to be recognized.

"Mom—"

Shirley set the glass down hard on the counter next to the sink. Still looking out the window, she said firmly, "Sweetheart, I don't know for sure what's wrong with Dad. He was doing okay before the funeral, but something happened there. It seemed like he . . . I don't know." She turned now and looked directly at Teresa. "I'm sorry, Teresa. I just didn't know how to answer your question."

Teresa wanted to give her mother a hug, tell her it was okay, but Shirley left the kitchen before Teresa could do so. For a second time, Teresa felt a rush of tears that she struggled to hold back. She had worked so hard today to try to make things nice. She had thought it would help. The only one who even noticed was John, and she had been so embarrassed that she couldn't even respond to him!

"Mom, wait—" Teresa hurried after her mother into the living room. But Shirley had already gone upstairs.

Chapter Twenty Eight

Jimmy lay slumped back in the chair, dozing lightly. Behind him came the soft sound of the door opening, followed by light footsteps entering the hospital room. He roused himself and sat up.

Dr. Parsons, the neurologist from Clayton City, stood reading the chart at the foot of Marriane's bed. He raised his eyes and grinned at Jimmy. "Those foam cushions don't make the best of beds, do they?"

Rubbing his eyes with the palms of his hands, Jimmy struggled to clear his head. "Not really. But then beggars can't be choosers, I guess." He stood, stretching to relieve his cramped muscles.

He watched the doctor move to Marriane's side as he began testing her reflexes, lifting her eyelids and shining his tiny flashlight into her pupils, checking for a response. "How is she doing, Doc?"

Dr. Parsons didn't answer right away, but continued with his exam. After a moment he straightened and sighed deeply. "Jimmy, you've been sitting next to this bed for over a week without a break. You really ought to go home and get yourself some real rest. I'd like to prescribe a mild sedative to help you along for a while. No big deal, just something to help you sleep a little better for now."

Jimmy persisted. "Doc, how is she doing?"

The doctor turned his eyes away and stared at the walls before turning to face the tired, wrinkled, and determined young man before him.

"Quite honestly," he said, "she seems a bit worse. In a case like this, there are no hard and fast answers. There aren't even any good guesses. I don't know what to tell you, except that at this point it's not very hopeful." He reached for an empty chair and sat before Jimmy, leaning forward with his hands clasped before him. "Look, can we sit down for a minute?"

Jimmy sank back into the chair he had so recently vacated and tried to push away the hollow panic growing in his stomach.

Dr. Parsons looked Jimmy squarely in the eyes. "When patients lose a large amount of blood, as Marriane did, and go into a coma, they tend to come out of it fairly quickly once their blood volume has been replaced, and things physiologically are brought back under control. We've done this for Marriane, and yet she hasn't responded. When patients don't respond to the treatment, and remain comatose for an extended period, often, when they do wake up, there is some damage to their system that was previously undetected. I'm talking about some brain damage, Jim. In addition, you also find weakened muscles and circulatory problems."

He paused to give Jimmy time to absorb it all, then continued. "What I am trying to say is that if Marriane woke up right now, there would almost certainly be some serious damage. We'd need to take rehabilitation measures. She wouldn't be the wife you had two weeks ago, Jim. She may not ever fully recover. Her continued state of coma and the lack of neurological response indicates that there was some sort of brain damage, and we can't begin to evaluate how much or what kind until she does wake up. Do you understand?"

Jimmy sat stone still, trying to sort out the words and the meanings. Finally, he said, "So, Marriane will be handicapped? Is that what you're saying?"

"Very possibly. Perhaps in ways that will mainly be physical. Perhaps . . . her thinking processes may not be the same. You may find yourself married to a woman who is no longer capable of functioning as a woman, or a wife."

The pounding in Jimmy's ears, he realized with a start, was his own heart racing. The words he had heard were incomprehensible to him. All this time, all these days, all he had hoped for, prayed for, was his Marriane to wake up, for things to get back to the way they were before. And now, they might never be the same. His head pounded and his ears rang. He suddenly felt dizzy with disbelief. This couldn't be happening!

The doctor reached over and touched Jimmy's arm gently. Jimmy tried to focus, and slowly, the concerned face of the doctor swam into clarity once more.

"Jimmy," came the gentle voice, "from all the vital signs that we've been watching, it's very possible that Marriane won't wake up. She seems to be slipping away from us, and there doesn't seem to be anything we can do to prevent it. Jimmy, I think you need to prepare yourself for her possible death."

Jimmy had thought he had already reached the end of his endurance before, at the thought of being married to a handicapped child for the rest of his life. But this, this was worse. Not to have Marriane at all? Suddenly, the thought of a handicapped Marriane was not so bad. The idea of a life without her at all was unthinkable, unbearable.

Through his shock, the doctor said, "I know it's painful, Jimmy, but you needed to know and prepare. And even though I've dumped all the worst case scenarios on you and even though these are real possibilities, still no one knows what will happen. And whatever happens, you can count on us to give Marriane the best possible care. I'll do everything I can for her, and for you. I want you to know that, Jim."

Jimmy raised his tear-streaked face to meet the troubled doctor's eyes. He reached out and grasped the doctor's hand. "Thank you, Dr. Parsons. You're a good man, and a good doctor. I know you've done everything. . . ." Jimmy started to sob, caught himself, and struggled on. "I appreciate it. We appreciate it. Thanks."

Dr. Parsons stood up. "If you decide you'd like those pills, I'll leave a prescription at the nurse's station for you. You can pick them up from the hospital pharmacy at any time."

Jimmy nodded acknowledgement, and without a word, the doctor left the room to continue his rounds.

The tears poured freely down Jimmy's face, dropping unheeded off his jaw and chin, running down his face. Eyes squeezed tightly shut, as if to keep out the awful truth, his stomach twisted into excruciating knots, he felt as if his heart would break.

Without thinking, he began to pray. "Oh my Lord, my God, help me. Help us! Help me receive the Comforter into my heart and find again my trust in Thee. Please . . . please guide me. Things are so bad, Lord, so much worse than I realized. I'm so frightened. Please God, I don't want to lose her. What do I do? What's going to happen now?"

He prayed long and hard, pouring out his heart as he never had before, or needed to. He had believed and loved God all his life, but never had he been asked to give up everything he cared for.

Much later that morning, emptied at last of tears and fear, Jimmy rose slowly, stiff and in pain. His face was calm, and peace was in his eyes. He had been to the mountain. He had laid Marriane on the altar of God.

He understood through his prayer what he would do. He knew now that he didn't need to know what to do about his beloved Marriane. The Lord would decide that. All he needed to know was what he, Jimmy, would do. And that, he now knew.

He loved Marriane. Not just for this life, but for all eternity. That was the promise he had made to her when he proposed; and then again made sacred in the temple as they were married for all eternity. As much as he loved her before, it was nothing compared to what he felt now. And he knew if she died, he would live his life as best he could and fulfill his time on the earth, until they could be reunited in heaven. And if she lived, well, whatever difficulties she brought with her, they would face together. The three of them—Marriane, he, and God, together. They would do it, whatever that meant, no matter what. He knew it, he believed it, and at last he was at peace and able to accept whatever came.

Smiling gently at the dearest person in his life, he leaned carefully over Marriane and kissed her softly on the forehead, on her closed eyes, on her still lips. Then, settling himself on the bed next to her, he took her hand in his and caressing her fingers began to sing softly, "I Need Thee Every Hour."

All was still.

Chapter Twenty Nine

"That should hold you for a while," Shirley said as she set the towering plate of pancakes down on the huge oak table. John waited until everyone else had a chance at the pancakes before he took two of them. He had spent the night at the Larson home, and he and Brent had been up early and out feeding the animals when Terrell had left for a bishopric meeting. As John cut into the pancakes on his plate, he said a silent prayer for the bishop this day.

As the Larson clan ate, Randy and Boyd wrestled over the last eight pancakes on the platter before Randy turned to little Amanda and said loudly, "Hey, Sis, how about passin' over the syrup?"

Amanda calmly and slowly got the syrup for her rowdy brothers and ignored their routine obnoxiousness. "Are you staying for Christmas, John?" Her big brown eyes looked up at him with pure innocence and hope.

John didn't answer immediately. It didn't look like he was going to be able to be here to celebrate and enjoy these people whom he loved so dearly. There were parts of his mission in town that were still undone, and they had to come first. But oh, how he longed to stay a while, a bit more, and be part of them a little longer. "You'd like that, wouldn't you?" he teased.

Amanda smiled and nodded her head. Then she got out of her chair and came over to John. "Please come to Christmas?" she pleaded as she hugged on his arm.

John's eyes filled with tears. These were the times that, in the long life he lived, were the hardest. He swiveled in his chair and picked her up to hold her close. "We'll see, little one," was all he could say.

* * *

The old pickup truck groaned and wheezed as Terrell drove toward the church house that Sabbath morning. Normally his thoughts were of the meetings and interviews his calling as bishop entailed each Sunday. But this time things were different. His mind couldn't shake what he had seen at Henrietta Turnsen's funeral. It was as clear now as it had been that day. He could still see Henrietta, encircled by light, standing in the midst of a soft sphere of glowing light that was all colors, and yet no color at all, a brightness that should have been too much to look at radiated out from a circle. She had been dressed in a dazzling white dress of simple but beautiful design. Her face had been rested and calm while her eyes were alive and sparkled with joy. Terrell had noticed how much younger she looked than she had at her death, or even all the years he had known her.

"I was allowed to come back this once to talk to you," she had spoken clearly to his mind and heart. "I came back to help you, Terrell. So listen to me carefully, cause I don't have much time. You need to completely let go of your anger at Jake Skoggins, right now."

"Before you died," Terrell had responded to Henrietta, speaking silently to her, "you taught me being angry only blocked the healing for whatever hurt happened to us in our lives. You showed me that no matter how deep, or . . . how long the hurt had gone on, God could take all that hurt and replace it with joy."

"That's right, Terrell," she had said, "That's what I told you. But you and I both know that you haven't fully let go of wanting to play God. You still think in your heart that Jake Skoggins must be punished before you can let go of what he did to Marriane. And you have no intention at all of forgiving him for the death of your granddaughter."

Henrietta's words still burned in Terrell's heart. He knew that all the truth he had learned these past years about having faith and trusting in God had come down to this one point in his life. Was he going to trust that all things really were in God's hands or wasn't he? Could he leave his desire for justice in the hands of an all-knowing, all-powerful God, or did he, Terrell, believe he had to do it all himself or it wouldn't get done?

Terrell's heart had cried out, "I—I want to follow the example you set for me. For all of us. It's just so hard! That little baby, my. . . !"

"Your granddaughter is here, with God. I've seen her! She is safe. She is happy." Henrietta had smiled broadly. "Terrell, nothing anyone does in anger to hurt us during life is beyond God's love to heal."

At that point, the vision of Henrietta had begun to fade. The sphere of light faded in on itself first, and then she herself became transparent. "Let go, Terrell" she said. "Let go and trust." Her words still lingered in his mind.

Pulling into the chapel parking lot, Terrell sighed deeply. He wished he could write off what he had seen at the cemetery that day as only so much stress and worry about Marriane. But he knew he couldn't. He had been given a message that he feared to ignore. If only it didn't mean he had to forgive what seemed so unforgivable, to love someone who seemed so unlovable.

Terrell turned off the truck, looked around the parking lot and noticing no one about, bowed his head in prayer. He sought the strength that only God could give him, the peace of spirit he had to have this day.

"Bless me, Lord, that I might be a better man than I am," he pleaded. "Help me rise above the smallness of my mind, that I might follow Thy example, and walk in Thy footsteps. I'm not as good or as strong as I'll have to be to do what Thou asks of me. My testimony is so much weaker than I ever thought it was before."

When he got out of the truck a while later, his step was a bit lighter and his vision clearer. He had passed through his own Gethsemane. He had taken another step upward and received the increase he had sought for.

* * *

This Christmas Eve fell on Sunday, and consequently guaranteed a greater turnout at church than usual. The hearts of those members of the Church who generally found an excuse to do something else on Sunday were more open to the prompting to come worship on such a day. Even if you didn't have the comfort of a daily relationship with

God, at this time of year it was at least easier to believe in some kind of benevolent power or influence in life. So even those most timid of testimony and the least open to the whisperings of the Spirit would come together at this time if only to take a break from the pressures of the world, from the turmoil and troubles of life. Putting aside for a few moments the differences between them, and letting in for a short time the thought that all people are of the same family, they would gather together in peace.

As sacrament meeting drew to an end, Bishop Larson rose to say a few words before the closing prayer.

"Sisters and Brothers, old and young, long-time members and new, those that are firm in the faith and those that are struggling, I speak unto you all.

"No matter what happens, or does not happen as you desired it to this Christmas, please know that Heavenly Father loves you. His love is so much more than we know. It goes beyond the furthest reaches of what we can imagine.

"Our Savior, Jesus Christ, was born to be the Way, the Truth, and the Life. He came to draw all of us unto Him, that He might guide us along the path that will lead us back home to our Celestial glory, our home with God. Along this path are the strengthening and shaping challenges we need to make us fit and capable to receive the Spirit of God, to make us able to live where God is, and become as He is.

"As we end this meeting and go to our homes, as we anticipate the gifts and goodies, as we enjoy the company of those we hold dear, let us remember, as it has been said that it is He who is the reason for the season. May God bless and keep you all."

Chapter Thirty

There wasn't much conversation in the darkened car as they rode together. Terrell and Shirley were in the front seat, John and Teresa in the back, with little Amanda in the middle. Amanda held on to John as if she thought he would run away if she didn't keep an eye on him.

These five were on their way to join Jimmy as he sat by Marriane's bedside. It had been eleven days since she had drifted into the coma, and except for the briefest of times, he had been at her side constantly. Their goal was to offer what comfort they could give to him and what love Marriane could feel from them. Amanda had pleaded so fervently to be allowed to stay up late and go "give Marriane a big hug to help her get better" that she had won her parents over.

"Amanda's too young," Teresa had warned. "The hospital staff's bound to say no." But John had assured the family it would be all right.

As they pulled into the hospital parking lot, Amanda nodded off completely. John took her in his arms and tenderly carried her into the hospital. Several staff members noticed them as they walked down the hallway toward Marriane's room, and seeing Amanda, one of the nurses stepped forward to halt John. But she stopped abruptly as if she had pushed against a door that wouldn't open. The quiet, peaceful feeling that came over her brushed aside her other concerns, and she stood and watched them pass.

They found Jimmy sitting quietly, gazing at his wife. Her wan face showed the stress of being comatose for so long. Jimmy felt worn, yet quiet and centered. Everyone kept their voice low to match the still mood in the room.

Terrell put his hands on his son's shoulders. "Jim, we've come to spend Christmas Eve with you two." Shirley came over to her son, and putting her cheek next to his, kissed him and whispered in his ear, "It's going to be okay. We're here."

Teresa had gone straight to Marriane and, finding the bedcovers somewhat amiss she had begun to straighten them. John still held Amanda in his arms, who now began to wake.

Terrell stepped over to Marriane and gently touched her cheek. As he stood beside the still form of his dear daughter-in-law, a lingering feeling of anger stirred up inside him. He turned slightly and looked at Jimmy, who was talking quietly to his mother. He saw his son's reddened eyes and pale face and wished there was something to be done.

When Terrell turned back to look at Marriane, he noticed John watching him from across the bed. Their eyes met and Terrell thought he heard John say, "Let your love be enough. Don't waste this time with anger. They need you too much for that." But of course, John hadn't spoken out loud.

Terrell strained against the pressure in his mind, against the tension in his stomach. When it seemed he would not prevail, a little hand slipped into his. Looking down, he saw his Amanda's innocent eyes looking up into his.

"Daddy, could we give Marriane her gift now?"

"What can we possibly give her?" asked Teresa in amazement.

Amanda looked at Marriane's lax face and said solemnly, "We can give her our love. That's what Jesus gives to us on Christmas." Looking up at her father, she asked, "Doesn't He, Daddy?"

"I'm sure she already knows we love her," Teresa protested.

"But we have to tell her tonight that we do," insisted Amanda.

"But honey, people in a coma can't hear what is being said to them," explained Teresa.

"Marriane can," Amanda said solemnly.

John spoke up gently, "Amanda is right. Marriane hears what we are saying. And she knows what we feel. She is able to perceive things better now in some ways than before she went into the coma."

"That's right," emphasized Amanda, "so we need to have a prayer and let her know we love her, like Jesus does." Reaching out to touch Marriane's still hand, she added, "That's what Jesus wants us to do, to help her be all better."

"I think that we should . . . ," another voice spoke up.

Everyone turned to look at Shirley. She reached out to take Terrell's hand, rose to stand beside him.

Terrell looked deeply into his beloved wife's eyes and found a strength he could draw from. Turning back to look down at Marriane, he said softly, "We do need to kneel and pray for her. That way she can know how much we love her." Almost as one, Terrell, Shirley, and Amanda knelt down beside the bed. Wordlessly, Teresa joined them. Jimmy and John knelt as well.

Terrell looked imploringly over at John, who shook his head slightly. Terrell closed his eyes and began to pray on behalf of them all. There was a sweet spirit in the room.

Afterwards, John stood to leave, although Amanda wouldn't let him until she had given him a big hug around his neck. "I'll miss you so much," she whispered. "I know you won't come see us for a long time."

John could see in her eyes that she knew. He squeezed her hand but did not try to reassure her falsely that it could be otherwise. In a few short months these people had become family to him. The eternal perspective that he enjoyed only served to heighten the deep attachment he felt for them. How could he begin to express that in the few moments left between them?

"I . . ." Tears filled his eyes as he tried to speak. "I love you all so much. You've taken me in and made me feel a part of your family. Thank you so much." One by one he embraced them, sometimes smiling, sometimes chuckling through his tears.

Teresa stepped back, as if by so doing she could blend into the wall, but John smiled at her as if he could read her mind. Pulling her toward him in a big hug, he whispered so softly that only she could hear, "You remember what we talked about—and don't forget I'm your friend. Always and forever." Then he winked at her as he stepped back, and quickly left the room. Teresa stood there, speechless, in stunned amazement.

When he had gone, Amanda turned back to Marriane and after stroking her hand for a while said, "You're going to be better real soon now. 'Cause we prayed about it."

Chapter Thirty One

The cold December air bit into his lungs as he walked along the road. It was way past sunset at this time of year, and except for the Christmas decorations and the lights of the homes he passed, the little town was dark.

John could hear Christmas music playing in one home nearby, and a party in another. He noticed, very faintly in the distance, hymns being sung at the Methodist church in a late Christmas Eve service.

John could imagine parents putting last minute touches on gifts for their children, and children snuggled down in bed, struggling to go to sleep so morning and presents would come quickly. This was a great time of year! If only it could be more like this all the time, he thought. John's heart was light and peaceful as he soaked in the spirit that emanated from all about him.

Then, sliding along on the fringes of his awareness, he felt a darkness, a queasy sensation, something similar to what someone would feel upon seeing a rat scurry along the wall while in church. The feeling of revulsion was all the more powerful because it had intruded so unexpectedly in the midst of such pleasant sensations.

His steps slowed a bit as he focused in on the negative . . . no, it was more than that; it was an evil presence. It was faint, but there was no mistaking what it was. He didn't know exactly what it was all about yet, but he knew where it came from. Now it was his task to get a clearer perception.

John stopped walking, straining to hone in on what he needed to do now. The Spirit always made him aware of such a presence, but it was often his own task to piece together the meaning. He stepped into that part of his being where a quiet and pure intent allowed the best communication with the Spirit, closed his eyes, and opened himself to receive any and all impressions that could be of help.

The thought that occurred to him jolted him out of his quiet. He didn't want to believe what the impression actually meant. But as he began walking again, the closer he got to his room at the boarding house the stronger came the evil feeling, and the more convinced he was of the truth of his impression. From the feeling in the pit of his stomach, he knew that a tragedy was in the making.

* * *

Jake Skoggins swore as his hand landed squarely on top of a nail point protruding from the eave of the roof. In the light of the half–moon through the clouds, he saw that the flesh near his thumb had been slashed as the deep, jagged wound began to bleed heavily.

It was just one more thing to blame on John. Jake felt everything that had gone wrong in his life lately was John's fault. Before John had come here, things had been all right. Jake had been respected. Well, maybe not respected, but he had been feared anyway, and in Jake's book, that was as good, if not better. But now he was laughed at openly whenever he went into the Happy Time Bar. He didn't have a job since Templeman had called the sheriff on him, and he had spent time in the county jail. Templeman would have been dog food if that John hadn't showed up!

Then the Larson baby died, and everyone blamed him for it. How was I to know she was pregnant? he thought. I just gave the car a lit-tle nudge. I only meant to throw a scare into them. Who knew the dumb little car would run into a tree? That kind of makes it their own fault!

Jake could have gone on like that, standing on the roof of the boarding house, hating John and justifying all the things he was doing to get even, but with the moon shining down, Jake realized that any-one going by on the street could see him standing on the roof. So he hurriedly scrambled along behind a gable to wait until the moon clouded over again.

When it looked okay to move, he came out of hiding. His hand hurt more and more. Each time he used it to climb, the rough asphalt shingles tore at the wound. In his other hand he clutched a bag that held the flares he had stolen from Templeman's store. They ought to make quite a show when he set them off in John's room!

A sheriff's patrol car drove down the street past the boarding house and lingered for a moment at the corner before going on. Jake broke into a cold sweat as his thoughts raced wildly in the fear he might be caught. After a while, when nothing happened and the car went on, he relaxed and began climbing along the roof again, searching for the room that was John's.

Someone began sneezing loudly inside the house and Jake froze. When he was satisfied that no one had noticed his movement on the roof, he continued. Finally he came to the window he had been looking for. Finding it unlocked, he quickly climbed into the room and silently closed the window.

Driven by curiosity and a perverted sense of power, Jake momentarily set aside the bag containing the flares and started going through the contents of the dresser drawers and the closet. He didn't know what he was looking for, but it was exciting to be able to do whatever he wanted with John's belongings, such as they were. There wasn't much of anything to find—a pair of jeans, a denim shirt, a woolen scarf, some soap, a towel, a razor, a toothbrush, and a book. Holding the book up in the dim light of the moon, he squinted at the pages and read haltingly out loud to himself: "'Wherefore, the guilty taketh the truth to be hard, for it cutt . . . cutteth them to the very center.'"

He didn't fully understand what that meant, but it gave him an uneasy feeling in his stomach. Turning to another place in the book, he continued reading: "'And our spirits must have become like unto him, and we become devils, angels to a devil, to be shut out from the presence of our God, and to remain with the father of lies, in misery, like unto himself; yea, to that being who . . . beguiled our first parents, who transformeth himself nigh unto an angel of light, and stirreth up the children of men unto secret com . . . comb . . . combinations of murder and all manner of secret works of darkness.'"

Slamming the book shut in disgust, Jake glanced at the cover:

The
BOOK
OF
MORMON
Another Testament
of Jesus Christ

As if he had touched a cobra, he quickly dropped the book to the floor and kicked it across the room. Then he had another thought. Retrieving the book, he sat down on the edge of the bed and began tearing pages out, one by one. This was going to be more fun than he had thought. He could start the fire from the pages of John's own "Holy Joe" book!

* * *

Homer Ballshide didn't have much to do this Christmas Eve. The people who occupied the rooms he rented out in his old, three-story house were as near to a family as he had ever come. Some of them had been living there for almost the whole twenty-three years he had been renting rooms, and he had come to know their routines and peculiarities at times better than they did themselves.

Homer hadn't liked many people in his lifetime, so most people hadn't liked him in return. He found most people to be pretty self-involved. But to be fair, he had to admit he was the same way. During the eighty years of his life he had mostly existed from one day to the next. He had felt awkward when John had started coming around and visiting with him in the evenings. However, as the weeks had passed, Homer had come to look forward to John's visits. When John had been occupied with other business and couldn't make his usual visits, Homer had felt something missing in his life. So it was with an anxious eye he had kept track of John's comings and goings.

Right now, Homer felt something was wrong. He could tell pretty accurately when something was not right in the old house, whether it be a mechanical, structural, or people problem. Climbing stiffly out of his easy chair, he grumbled under his breath about his arthritis and slid his pale, blue-veined feet into his slouch slippers. Pulling his belt more tightly around his robe, he slowly made his way over to turn off the television before opening the door of his own quarters.

Homer had a routine he always followed to check his house. After listening at his own door, he locked the door behind him and began to patrol the halls and stairways.

By the time he reached the third floor he was breathing heavily. His legs were wobbly and his heart felt like it would burst out of his chest. The strong sense that something was wrong had propelled him along faster than usual, but it hadn't given him any more energy.

He listened at Clyde Filben's door and could hear his regular, shrill snore. Sure glad he sleeps way up here, thought Homer. Then he made his way down the hallway to John's room, carefully avoiding the board that always squeaked when someone stepped on it. I know he hasn't come back yet, thought Homer, 'cause he always stops by to say hello if my light is on. So it can't be here where the problem is.

Homer had already turned back when he heard it. A funny kind of sound, sort of like . . . paper tearing. There was no light showing under the door, and since John wasn't back, there shouldn't have been anyone in the room. Homer listened closely and heard a muffled laugh. Silently pushing open the door, he stood a few seconds in the dark doorway before flicking on the light. Jake jumped like he had been stuck with a pitchfork.

"What are you doing here?" demanded Homer.

Jake stood still, the mutilated book forgotten in his hand. His mind was feverishly trying to react to this unexpected interruption when the old man declared, "I'm calling the police!"

Everything happened in a blur. Homer turned to go and Jake dropped the book, lunged at him, and grabbed the old man's robe. There was a tearing sound, and both men fell forward heavily to the floor in the doorway.

Jake rose to his knees and rolled the old man over, raising a fist to strike him. As the limp body rolled loosely in his hands, he dropped his fist. He thought Ballshide was probably still alive, just uncon- scious. Taking his victim by the arm and the belt of his robe, Jake dragged him inside and shut the door.

Jake had only loosely planned what he would do once he got into John's room. Now he had to figure out what to do with the old man as well. "Stupid old man! What did you go and stick your face in here for?" growled Jake. He clenched his fist, wanting to hit the frail old body out of frustration, but decided it was useless. Then Jake realized

Homer could identify him. What was he going to do with him now?

He looked around, then grabbed Homer's robe and took the belt out of it. Using it like a rope, he tied the old man's hands behind his back, then dragged him over to the closet and shut him in.

I'll do somethin' with him later. Somethin', thought Jake. The thought faded as soon as he had experienced it.

* * *

John had not been running toward the boarding house, but he wasn't walking slowly either. The closer he approached, the more clear was his understanding of what was going on. He knew Jake was there. He also knew the people who lived there were in danger. The particulars of how all that would come together were still coalescing in his mind.

At the front door of the boarding house, John stopped and listened. The image of Homer tied up and tucked into the closet in John's room came to his mind. The vision of the gash on the old man's cheek added to John's concern. But how to get everyone out and safe before it was too late?

Should I wake everyone on my way up to the third floor, he wondered, or would that get them frightened and make a lot of noise Jake would hear? I don't want to scare him into making things worse. I'm the one he wants; everyone else is just incidental.

John decided to go straight up. As he climbed the flights of stairs, he quieted his mind and heart so he would be ready for whatever came. For himself he had no fear; his own life would not end until his mission here upon the earth was complete. No power of man could harm him, nor stop his work and mission for the Lord. John's concern was for Jake and Homer and the innocent, sleeping people in the boardinghouse.

When he got to the third floor, he walked down the hall past Clyde's snoring and deliberately stepped on the squeaky board. As it filled the silent hallway with its complaint, John heard a slight movement in his room. He noisily put his key in the lock and opened the door, to let Jake know he was there.

Behind the door, Jake tensed, waiting for John. He had no intention of giving his opponent a fair chance; John had somehow beaten him before. Now Jake hoped to use his greater weight and bulk to knock John off his feet. After that, Jake figured he knew enough to win.

John came into the room, and before he could turn on the light, Jake jumped him. The two of them flew across the room and slammed into the dresser before going down. John turned to look at Jake just as Jake struck him; immediately he went limp. Jake had already started to strike again when he realized the fight was already over. His relief was mixed with disbelief. Part of him didn't believe his opponent could be beaten that easily. Jake backhanded John across the face and shook him a little, but got no response.

Satisfying himself that that battle had been won, Jake dragged John over to the bed and threw him on it. Taking a roll of duct tape from his bag, he began to bind John to the bed. He passed the roll under the bed and over John time after time.

Jake had only the crudest of plans. After he had secured John to the bed, he would use the flares to set fire to the room. When things were burning really well, and John was begging Jake to let him go, then Jake would at last have his revenge. Maybe he would let him loose, maybe he wouldn't.

Jake was just picking up the last two flares to put in place around the bed when he heard, "It's still not too late, you know."

Jake whirled around. The moonlight through the window illuminated John's face. "I can still help you, Jake," said John.

"You can't help nobody," snarled Jake. He was suddenly afraid again, afraid of a power he felt, didn't understand, and knew was greater than his had ever been. Cramming one of the flares into his back pocket, he pulled the lid off the top covering on the other one and scratched it alive. As the bright orange and white flame shot out he said, "You're not so tough. There ain't goin' to be nothing left of you but ashes!"

John had let himself be restrained, hoping that he would be able to talk to Jake, to reach him, find some place of softness in his heart. As John continued to speak to Jake, the Spirit did find some small places to work on, and there was some softening in the frightened man. A tiny little part of him did not want to do this awful thing, but it was too weak to overthrow the angry, fearful part.

" . . . all the pain that you feel, all the troubles in your life, can be fixed. I'll help you. That's why He came, that's why He lived for us all."

It's hard to say in what way it might have happened differently, had Clyde Filben not been awakened by the smell of smoke from the flare. It wasn't a lot of smoke, and most people wouldn't even have noticed it, but Clyde had the kind of large, wide-nostriled nose that picked up on smoke. Awakened from his routine snoring with a snort, Clyde sat bolt upright in bed. His eyes blinked twice, he sniffed a moment, then jumped out of bed and burst out of his room yelling at the top of his lungs. "FIRE!!! FIRE!!! Someone CALL THE FIRE DEPARTMENT!! CALL the SHERIFF!!!" Then he ran down the hall, barely managing the stairs as he tripped on his long nightshirt with bare, size 14 feet, banging on every door in the boardinghouse.

Jake reacted to Clyde's yelling as if he had been jabbed with a cattle prod. His face immediately tightened back up, and his eyes once again focused on John. Jake's last chance to make a different choice seemed to be gone.

John saw this and knew what it meant. Sitting up, he reached for Jake, and as he did, the duct tape fell off of him as if it had been made of tissue paper.

Jake reacted blindly and dropped the burning flare onto the bed. The intense flame from the flare immediately ignited the bed covering, melting the duct tape. As the flames engulfed the bed, John rose calmly to stand before Jake, completely unafraid.

Jake snapped! He went crazy inside and lighting another flare, stumbled out of the room, shouting, "I'm going to burn this whole place down!" He ran down the hallway and careened down the stairs.

John knew Jake was setting fire to anything that would burn as he ran wildly through the house, the lighted flare in his hand. It would not take long before the old place would be completely engulfed in flames. Shaking off the last of the tape, he went to the closet and pulled Homer out of it. The old man was moaning slightly, and John took a quick moment to touch the wound on Homer's face before picking him up in a fireman's carry and taking him out of the flame-filled room.

Chapter Thirty Two

The Larsons drove home quietly from the hospital, each lost in their own thoughts and feelings. Amanda slept in the back seat with her head on Teresa's lap. Shirley sat in the middle of the front seat next to Terrell as he drove. His mind was still turning over the events of these past days when the sound of the Crystal Volunteer Fire Department siren split the peaceful Christmas Eve.

As Terrell was a member of the fire department, he automatically brought the car around and headed toward the town hall, beside which was the garage where the fire truck was kept. In a small town like this everyone helped each other, if for no other reason than because you never knew when it would be you that needed help. But he hadn't gone very far when the fire truck met him going in the other direction, so he turned the car around again to follow behind.

Even before they got to the boarding house, Terrell could see the smoke filling the night air. Knowing that John lived there, and the old place was as big a fire trap as any he knew of, Terrell gave a swift prayer that they could get everyone out safely.

As he pulled up behind the fire truck in front of the boarding-house, Seth Templeman came running up. His breath was choppy and his face was flushed. "Okay Larson, what have we got here?" he gasped out. Seth had been a volunteer fireman longer than anyone else and was the unofficial chief by seniority.

"Don't know, just got here myself," Terrell replied as he got out of the car. He pulled off his sports coat and tossed it back into the car, then leaned over and kissed Shirley on the cheek. Then he hurried with Seth to the fire truck to coordinate with the others, who were already unrolling hoses and setting up.

At the sight of the boardinghouse residents huddled together before the burning building, Shirley turned toward Teresa in the back seat and said, "I'm going to go see what I can do to help. Keep an eye on Amanda." Then she was out of the car and gone in the dark before her daughter could answer. She could see that most of the residents were poor and elderly, and had not had time to grab much in the way of warm clothing.

Smoke and flames poured from the windows of the three-story house. Over the shouts of the fire crew could be heard the sound of glass shattering as windows exploded from the heat. There was almost nothing left of the third story around back where John's room had been. The fire crew quickly hooked up hoses to the fire hydrant down the street and began shooting water towards the upper stories.

Harry Morse and the sheriff arrived about the same time. Harry turned off the ignition, jumped out, and hit the ground running all in one movement. Terrell saw him coming and threw him a coat. "Come with me, we'll try the front door," he yelled. Harry grabbed an ax off the truck, put on his fire hat and ran after Terrell, boots in hand.

As they got to the front steps, there was a crash and a part of the porch roof came plummeting down. It swung through the front glass window, shattering it into a million pieces. Terrell and Harry jumped out of the way to avoid the deadly destruction, and in so doing lost their footing. When they rolled over on the ground and looked in the hole that used to be the window, they saw a sight that chilled their blood. John stood in the house, surrounded by fire. He had someone draped over his shoulders.

* * *

As he carried the unconscious Homer along on his shoulders, John had stopped to check each tenant's room to make sure it was empty. Clyde had done a good job; everyone was already gone, although a few had been reluctant to believe such an inconvenient message of trouble on this Christmas Eve night. It was cold outside, and besides, Clyde had thought he'd seen a flying saucer last year, and Bigfoot the year before that. But the unmistakable smell of smoke had convinced them all.

As John made his way through the doomed house, he saw that Jake had done his work of arson well. Besides the main fire on the third floor, there were many smaller blazes that hungrily ate up the aged, dry wood, making it impossible for a small-town fire crew with antiquated equipment to save the house.

It had taken so much time to make sure everyone was gone that by the time John got to the ground floor, his way was blocked by a wall of fire. He knew that Homer was coming around and would need medical attention soon.

"You thought it was over, didn't you!" yelled someone from behind him. John spun around to see Jake coming at him with a burning two-by-four in his hand.

Just then, a part of the porch roof gave way. John fell to the floor, Homer falling with him. John staggered to his feet, picking Homer up again. Jake had disappeared in the burning rubble.

"John!" yelled Terrell, trying to be heard above the roar of the flames. "Come around by the front door and we'll get you out!" As he and Harry rushed to break open the door, he gasped, "I hope!"

The two axes made short work of the door. They had to jump aside as flames shot out of the doorway and made it impossible to see inside.

"We have to get the Number Two hose over here or we'll never get him out," shouted Harry over the roar of the fire.

"John! Stay put! We have to get a hose to cover you through the flames!" yelled Terrell over the roar of the fire.

They were still getting the Number Two hose to take back with them from the fire truck when John walked up beside them and set Homer down on the ground. "Here, one of you take him for me and see he gets some care. He got knocked on the head pretty good."

"How did you get out of there?" Terrell blurted. "There was no way. We . . . how did you get out of there?"

John shook off the question. "It doesn't matter."

"But I thought you— "

John grabbed Terrell by the shoulders in a crushing grip. "The house can't be saved. Jake Skoggins set fire to it in too many places for you to do anything about it."

Terrell growled, "That figures. More people hurt by that creep!"

"I have to go back in and get him out," John said quietly.

"What!" exclaimed Terrell. "You're going back in for that low life? Maybe this is the justice he de—"

"Don't say it, Terrell," warned John over the noise around them. "This is my concern now, not yours!" He loosened his grip on Terrell and smiled warmly. "You've been thinking you knew who I am, so let that be enough reason why I have to go back in, and why you have to let it go. I—"

A cloud passed over John's face though his eyes were bright. Turning back to look at the house, he murmured. "Oh, Jake." Then he said urgently to Terrell, "It's going to explode. You need to get everyone well away from it!"

"What—? Why—?" stammered Terrell.

John gave Terrell a little push. "I don't have time to explain. Just trust me. You need to get everyone well away from it! Remember, no matter what happens, I love you, Terrell, and God loves you." Then he was gone back to the house, leaving Terrell staring after him.

The glow of the burning house lit up one side of Terrell's face while the other reflected the Christmas lights from the house across the street. He was unsure of what to do, then he remembered to listen to his heart, and the balance tipped to one side.

"Seth! Sheriff! We need to get everybody away from the house," he hollered.

* * *

Jake had barely missed being crushed by the burning debris as he had charged John with the fiery two-by-four, and the roof had come crashing through the front window. His escape was not complete, though. A burning splinter from one of the rafter beams had shot out and driven itself into his right eye. Nothing in his life could have prepared him for the degree of sheer agony he felt. He staggered down a hallway that crackled and popped with the fire he himself had set, and mirrored the searing pain in his blinded eye. In his lurching about, he tripped over a box of something that had been discarded in the hurried exodus from the burning house. He flung out his hands to check his fall over the box, but the weight of his body crashed through the cellar door in front of him and he plummeted headlong down the musty stairs.

John walked through the flames as though they weren't even there. "Jake!" he called over and over. Most of the time John could feel where people in pain were; but sometimes, when there was so much suffering all around him, it didn't work as well. *He doesn't deserve to die this way. No one does,* he thought. "Jake!"

A little prompting, a hunch, a passing thought touched John and evaporated. He saw the cellar doorway and the thought came to him, *like a wounded animal running into his cave.* Sidestepping the burning walls that were collapsing all around him, he made his way to the cellar doorway and started down.

* * *

At first no one had believed Terrell, but the force of his conviction about the explosion and his reputation for down-to-earth steadiness got through. Seth got the fire crew to put down their hoses and join the boardinghouse residents as they stood with the neighborhood onlookers down the street. The neighborhood residents had been quickly evacuated from their homes, and there was some grumbling going on about having to stand around in the cold. The sheriff and his deputy were keeping order as the crowd milled around and talked while they waited for the explosion that only Terrell knew anything about.

Teresa and Amanda sat in the car down the block, where Teresa had moved it away from the house. "John's in the house," said Amanda quietly as she looked out the car window at the house fire, "and he's looking for someone." Teresa took Amanda's hand in hers and squeezed it tightly.

"I don't think so, honey. The sheriff has everyone away from there. I guess they're afraid there's going to be an explosion."

"Yes, he is," insisted Amanda, "and he just found the man that's hurt in there."

Together they watched and waited.

* * *

John made his way carefully down the cellar stairs. The power lines had been destroyed and it was dark. Only the flickering of fire behind him gave off any light. The stair boards were loose and creaked with every step, and the grit and dust everywhere testified that this was a place rarely visited. He stepped around the new gas water heaters Homer had been installing.

"Jake? Jake, I know you're down here. I know you're hurt. Let me help, it's not too late."

"Stay away from me!" came a snarling response from behind some crates.

John slowly made his way toward the direction of the voice. Suddenly, the crates were pushed over on top of him. John barely had time to roll with the impact and avoid most of the weight of the dangerous trap.

"Ever since you came, everything's been messed up!" screamed Jake.

John rose to his feet from where he had fallen and saw for the first time the wound in Jake's eye. "Oh Jake, let me help you. That eye, it needs help."

"Stay away from me!!" cried Jake. The waves of pain, both physical and spiritual, washed over him again and again. His reason was gone, and all he could understand was the agony of the present. At that moment, he was more like a rabid dog than a human being.

John came slowly toward Jake with his arms outstretched. Jake picked up a rusty old ax and began swinging it around his head in circles as a protection, but the weight of it sent him staggering. As he did, the ax swung low and slammed into a new gas line against the cellar wall. Immediately, gas fumes began shooting into the cellar space.

John was the first to understand what had happened, then Jake roused somewhat from his pain-soaked fog. "We're goin' to die, and I'll see you in hell! This whole place is going up!" Almost without conscious thought, he scratched the last flare into life. There was a quick sensation of heat and pressure, then only blackness.

Chapter Thirty Three

Shirley stood by Terrell. The two of them waited, arm in arm, dirty and tired, their eyes focused on the house. Harry Morse and Seth Templeman stood together with the sheriff in front of the large crowd of people that had gathered. There was little talk as everyone watched and waited.

Janet Morse and her son Nathan had just driven up to the end of the block, when it happened. The sound of the explosion startled her so that her foot slipped off the clutch and the car jumped forward and stalled.

The blast from the ignited gas line demolished what was left of the Ballshide boardinghouse. Nevertheless, most of the impact was vertical rather than horizontal, in a way that investigators would later find very curious and unusual. Although several people who stood nearby were thrown back by the force of the explosion, and pieces of burning wood and glass were flung the full area of the block, no one was seriously injured. Neither was there much property damage to the surrounding homes.

After the initial shock of the explosion passed, all those who knew and loved John stood in shocked disbelief. It was as if they wished to stop time, and not go on to the next minute of life. If time ran on, it would require them to accept what had happened.

In that timeless moment when mortality and eternity touched, and the silence of their hearts filled them, the long overdue snowflakes began to fall. They were the kind of big, lazy snowflakes that take forever to hit the ground but keep piling up until there are mountains of snow. The kind of snowflakes that bury everything with a blanket of quiet, pure white.

Epilogue

Two days after the fire at the boardinghouse, a day after Christmas, Jimmy sat silently next to Marriane's bed, reading his scriptures as the winter sun sent a warm tendril of light through the ice-frosted window, and across the bed. The usual hospital undercurrent was missing this morning; even the noise from the hallway was reduced, and the room was filled with a peaceful quiet.

Marriane's eyes slowly fluttered open. At first, all she could make out was a blur of light. She lay quietly, blinking, struggling to focus. As her vision cleared, she could make out Jimmy sitting next to the bed, his head turned away from her, his profile outlined clearly in the morning light. He seemed an angel from heaven. She slowly stretched her hand out towards him, rustling the bedding as she did so.

Jimmy raised his head at the sound, turning towards her, his eyes opening wide as he saw her awake, her face filled with love as she reached for him. His breath caught, and he was almost unable to comprehend that she had awakened. Then suddenly, he fell from the chair onto his knees beside her. Gathering her gently, oh, so gently, into his arms, he pulled her close to him, and held her as if he would never let her go.

Her arms moved to encircle him, and that was how Dr. Parsons found them when he walked through the door a few moments later.

* * *

Marriane's recovery was slow. As Dr. Parsons had warned, there had been some neurological damage, similar to a stroke. It was determined later she had suffered the damage during or immediately after the surgery, which had compounded her existing complications and added to the length of the coma.

However, with rigorous physical therapy, priesthood blessings, prayers, and the support and love of her husband and family, she had determinedly worked. After a few months only a slight limp troubled her as she walked unaided. Her mental capacities had not been impaired. Her speech was only slightly slurred.

At the baby's memorial service, she sat in a wheelchair, and told the congregation she had seen her little one, named Shirley after her grandmother. And that she knew if she and Jimmy and lived up to their covenants in this life, their child would be restored to them.

Eighteen months after the accident, Jimmy and Marriane were blessed with a new infant son. They named him John, after their friend.

* * *

Nathan Morse ran away from home again, two weeks after Christmas. He left his parents a note, telling them that although he did love them, he couldn't live the way they did. He wanted to try life on his own, to be free to experience whatever he chose, freely and without interference. He promised to come back someday.

Bits and pieces of news about him drifted back from time to time. The last message Harry and Janet had said he was somewhere in California.

* * *

Janet Morse gave birth to a beautiful, healthy baby daughter on Christmas Day. She was a cherished blessing in their lives, and a solace to their wounded hearts when Nathan left.

A month after the fire, two weeks after Nathan left, Harry and Janet were visited by some friends of John's. The two clean-cut young men, dressed in suits, ties, and white shirts, brought a message of love and hope to their home that was most welcome. Three months after their first visit with the elders, Harry and Janet were baptized and began their lives anew as members of The Church of Jesus Christ of Latter-Day Saints. A year later, they were sealed in the temple with their little daughter, and their home became a true heaven on earth. John remained a special focal point in their hearts.

* * *

Seth Templeman softened over time. No one could ever accuse him of being a pushover, but his heart was more open and generous, his language kinder. He often was the first to offer help or donations wherever needed. He opened his heart and drew closer to those who befriended him, and he in turn befriended others. Sometimes he went to church, and finally allowed himself to cry and grieve openly for his wife. In so doing, his pain and loss began to heal. He drew closer to God, as he knew Him, and found greater peace and happiness than ever before.

* * *

Homer Ballshide recovered from the injuries he received the night of the fire, and was able with the insurance money to rebuild. He never forgot John, whose example inspired Homer to be more kind and accepting of others. He and Seth became good friends, and got together regularly for dinner and chess.

* * *

One evening after dinner, Teresa Larson was helping her mother clean up the kitchen. She brought up a subject that had been on her mind for weeks.

"Do you think John is alive?"

Shirley stopped wiping the dish in her hands and turned to look at her daughter. Teresa's face was troubled, her brows furrowed in concentration.

"What brought that up? I thought you didn't like John."

Teresa struggled to appear nonchalant. "Oh, I wouldn't say I didn't like him, he was just always underfoot. It got to be kind of annoying. But Mom, the night of the fire, it was pretty obvious that John must have been killed, yet you and Dad talk like he must have somehow survived. I don't understand it."

Shirley searched Teresa's face. Life was so hard for her. Teresa's faith was limited to the things she could see and touch and hear with her mortal body. Order and control were more important to feeling secure than trusting in God. Shirley dearly loved her oldest daughter, and it pained and tugged at her heart to know how much she would struggle and suffer in life until she could learn to trust others—especially God.

"Sweetheart, you spent plenty of time around John. What did you think of him?"

Teresa's cheeks flushed red with confusion as she sorted through her feelings and thoughts. "I don't know, he was nice, sort of. But different than other guys his age. I mean, I always thought he was about my age. But he didn't act like it. He always seemed to know what I, uh, what people were thinking and feeling. Like he could read your mind. It was kind of spooky, even kind of creepy at times. Definitely different."

"But you liked him?" her mother asked gently.

Teresa's heart felt funny and pulled within her. To her surprise a tear leaked out of the corner of her eye. "Yes," she said softly, "I liked him. Oh Mother, I'm so confused. He drove me crazy, always turning things around inside of me and changing the way the world looked. He used to make me so mad. How can I miss him so much?" The dam broke inside her and she sobbed into her hands. Feelings she had denied even to herself poured out now.

Shirley cradled her daughter in her arms, gently rocking back and forth as she had when Teresa had been a baby.

"Oh, my darling daughter. My little Martha. Bless your heart. Sweetie, growing and opening our hearts is so often a painful thing, just like childbirth. But it's worth it."

Sniffling, Teresa pulled back a bit. "Why did you call me Martha? Who's Martha?"

"I was talking about Martha, the sister of Mary and Lazarus in the New Testament. You've often reminded me of her. She was a good organizer; so are you. Both of you are very good at keeping things going as they should, all the little details. And just like Martha, as the Savior said, 'thou art careful and troubled about many things.' Lovey, keeping things in order is important, but the most needful thing is keeping our hearts open to the Spirit of the Lord, and to others. That often means nothing goes as we thought it would, or should—especially our relationships with people. But if we accept this, and lean on our Father in Heaven to guide us, we can not only survive, but thrive and find the greatest joy in life."

"What does this have to do with John?"

"John knew this, and tried to give that gift to you. If there were anything I could give you, my dear, it would be that trust and faith in God that John had. From that he knew how to live as he did. It means more than all the clean houses and organized offices in the world!" She hugged Teresa tightly. "That's why I called you my little Martha!"

Teresa sniffed, and wondered over what her mother had said. She didn't understand it, not really, not yet, and part of her wondered if she shouldn't be offended by being called a Martha, but her heart was soft right then, opened by her pain. What her mother had said might be true. She tucked it inside to ponder.

Pulling back, she reached into her pocket and withdrew a tissue to wipe her eyes and nose. She worked to regain her composure. Her mother watched quietly, praying in her heart that this might be the beginning of Teresa's heart opening up.

"Are you all right, honey?"

Teresa nodded, stuffing her tissue back into her pocket. "I'm okay. Mom, do you think he'll ever come back?" She had somehow accepted in her heart that John was alive, crazy as that might sound. She didn't understand how that could be, but she wanted it to be true.

"I don't know. But I know wherever he is, he'll always be our friend. John never forgets, I know that. So who knows? Perhaps we will see him again, sometime. Only God knows for sure."

With a tremulous smile, and a bit of comfort in her heart, Teresa reached out to give her mother one last hug before they returned to the ordinary business of living.

Later that evening, Shirley related to Terrell her conversation with Teresa, and her feeling about it. They were glad for yet another miracle, no matter how small, that John had wrought among them. In prayer they thanked God for sending him into their lives.

Their love had grown through the crucible of pain and fear. Purified more fully in the refiner's fire of their lives, their faith shone brighter and brighter, and their love one for another grew along with it. Out of their abundance they shared with those around them.

Terrell found courage, faith and trust enough to leave his unanswered questions about the suffering that comes through life in the Lord's hands. He came to understand it does all work out, in God's way and time. Telling others about it, and testifying to them that, "I don't know all the reasons, but I know it's true" became as natural a part of him as breathing.

* * *

Very little was ever found of Jake Skoggins. The force of the explosion left only a few bone fragments and half of a lighter with his name roughly scratched on it. Under a headstone paid for by the county, these few remaining traces of his life were buried in a small box. Terrell, Shirley, Jimmy, and Marriane leave flowers on occasion.

* * *

No trace of John was ever found in the remains of the boarding house. A memorial service was held for him but it left most who attended it still feeling unsettled. For weeks after the tragedy, one at a time, and often meeting each other unexpectedly, those who loved him and last saw him enter the house would come to stand by its remains and wonder.

There would not have been a good way to explain it all. Some things have to be left alone until the time is right. So even as the first light of Christmas Day was tapping on snow-covered windows in the little town of Crystal, a solitary man in a denim jacket and jeans walked across the bridge toward somewhere else. He had eyes that were filled with many years of living. His heart was sad at having to leave yet another place and people he had come to know and love. No one there would ever see him again in this life. But they would never forget John, either.

ABOUT THE AUTHOR

Thomas D. Eno has been a practicing counselor for over twelve years. He has served as Mental Health Director for several counties in three states. His diverse and varied experience has enabled him to understand, help, and relate to people of differing backgrounds and needs.

Thomas enjoys music, history, martial arts, and nature, as well as telling puns, laughing, and spending time with his wife, Laurie, and family.